MW01679499

LOSING THE FIGHT

EVERGREEN GROVE, BOOK FIVE

Elisabeth Staab

Cover photography by Period Images
Cover Model: Sean Hampton
Cover design by Babski Creative Studios
Editing by Kelli Collins

Book Layout ©2013 BookDesignTemplates.com

Book Ordering Information:
Quantity sales and special discounts are available. For details, contact the publisher at the email address above.

Losing the Fight/ Elisabeth Staab -- 1st ed.
ISBN 978-0-9971366-7-8

To sensitive alpha males everywhere for being so awfully damn lovable.

To Amber Belldene, Kristin Miller, and Robin Covington for being completely awesome.

Thank you.

PROLOGUE

Ty – Then

The fight hadn't even started, but it was already over.

I pressed my lips together as I checked my hand wraps, turning my back on the bag of slime snarling at me from two feet away in the locker room. "Get out of here, old man. I like to be alone before a fight. You don't belong here, and the sight of you makes me sick."

Arlo Specter was the sorriest excuse for a human. Affable and influential to the general public, and predatory here in these overheated, behind-the-scenes stone and metal rooms. His work as a boxing promotor had allowed him to get his hooks into my brother. This wasn't a boxing match and I refused to let him hook me.

"Look, Thacker, that film crew I sent over yesterday said you refused to give them an interview. Your brother and I had a deal and this shit's nonnegotiable. That whole orphan from a craphole town who becomes a UFC title holder shtick? People goddamn eat up those kinds of sob stories."

This guy could take his nonnegotiable and jump off a cliff for all I cared. My grandmother had taught me to respect my elders, but this guy would be lucky if I didn't break his face.

"Well damn, *Specter,* thanks for pointing out how lucky I am to be an orphan from a craphole town and all. That great stuff aside, your deal is with my brother like you said. And the deal is done. You're going to leave us both alone, starting now."

Some dude with headphones and a clipboard stuck his head in and motioned from the open locker room door. "Time to go."

Specter stops me with a hand to my shoulder that I immediately shake off. "Don't be stupid. You think you got to where you are all on your own? You think your brother did?" His smile turned dark and oily. "You should be a lot more grateful, Tyler."

For only a second I stuck an angry finger in his face before snatching it back. Don't wanna get too close to this guy. "You're disgusting. I'm not grateful. And I don't want your help."

"Careful. I've got more pull in this business than you realize, and if you keep picking at scabs it won't only be you who suffers."

Maybe he's right. The thing is, it burns deep to think that maybe I got to where I am because someone else helped move the pieces to get me here. And Terrence? Nah. No way. My brother never should have had to do what he did to get us ahead. After everything we've struggled for, he'd tell me not to be stupid… I felt like I finally had my head clear.

I'm wouldn't be playing any part of this shady deal any longer.

While the old man was too busy foaming and spitting to answer, I walked out to the cage. My heart thumped, calm and steady, in time to my steps down the long hall. I was ready.

The thing was, I started fighting to give myself a sense of control over a life that had so little. Finding out someone else had been lying to me? Pulling the strings of my career behind the scenes? Messing with my brother? No fucking way.

I'd rather lose this fight than let some asshole manipulate me or anyone I care about one more minute.

When Marques and I face off there's an eerie hush. Usually the fans are screaming, but for a moment after we touch gloves there's quiet. Or maybe it's that funny, muffled sensation in my head. That surreal sense that I'm breaking free from reality.

Because even as the fight progresses—as my pulse kicks up and as I grapple with my opponent for show—I know I'm going down. Marques is a good fighter. For one round and then another I hang in there, throwing punches without my usual speed but enough to make it look good.

My perfect chance comes at the end of the second round when Marques takes me to the mat, and gets in some hard as hell punches. Not exactly smiling through the pain, but I had the energy to fight back harder than I was.

Then my head bounced on the mat. Easiest thing ever to play up how much the hit stunned me. A white-out of my vision cleared to reveal Arlo Specter standing outside the cage with murder on his face as the ref called the fight.

He knew I did it on purpose. I didn't care. In fact, I wanted him to know.

Still down, I turned and gave him a smile.

In your face, asshole. Nobody controls me. Nobody fucks with my family. So take your bulging neck vein and your just desserts and choke on them.

"You sonovabitch!" He yelled. "I'll make sure you never fight again. You're finished."

Fine. Right now I'd rather go back to being broke. This satisfaction, it's bittersweet. My brother might not understand and already things between us are tense. But this, I can't do it anymore.

One day, I hope he'll recognize I did this out of love. Maybe I can even have a career again. Who knows.

I blow past Specter after the fight is called, this time ignoring him entirely when I stride back into the locker room. Someone's pushed a weight rack into the corner and I shove it across the door to keep him from getting inside. Old man's not strong enough to push it open.

My cell phone buzzes from the towel I left it sitting on. *Text message from Kate.*

I smile, the heavy throb in my head feeling better already. We've got plans tomorrow, and I shouldn't be looking forward to them but I am.

Kate: *Is everything okay? How did the fight go?*

Ty: *Exactly the way I planned*

1. TOO PRETTY FOR JAIL

Kate

Sometimes I think I've been trying to kill myself since the day I died. If you stay high, you never have to fall. Right?

Except everybody falls. Eventually.

"Kate, over here! Over here!"

I'm on a stage—if you can even call it a stage—at a field party in the middle of absolutely nowhere. Well…somewhere. I don't even know because I rode practically across three laps in the back of some guy's car, and we drank a deceptively sweet red alcohol mix along the way.

All I know now is I'm spinning my shirt on my finger, reveling in the cold night air on my goose-bumpy skin. My "bandmate," some guy with a guitar I met by the T-shirt tent, is pointing and telling me which way to toss the thing like a good enabler would.

Nice guy. Sam? Steve? I wonder if he has a car.

"All right, people, I'm putting this thing back on unless you tired sons of bitches can make a lot more noise!" Tonight I don't have a headache so the party sounds liven me up.

It's a decent crowd at this event. A few hundred people. The DJ had a cable short out and folks were getting restless without music, so I was happy to provide. Music isn't my lifelong career passion so much as my security blanket, I guess. I think singing through the pain is how I've kept from screaming. It's helped me to cut loose, like I am right now.

I miss having a real band, but Sam— or is it Sean?—is doing okay up here. And things are way livelier since we hijacked the sound system.

I lean over to whatzisname. "Hey, you can do 'Bad Reputation,' right?"

"Bitch, I can do that in my sleep."

"Let's go then."

Emo boy hunches over his guitar, and I fling my shirt into the crowd. My sports bra covers the worst of my scars, and darkness blankets me from all sides. I still get an adrenaline buzz from this every time. Someone could see. Someone could judge and call me ugly.

Fuck 'em.

The notes form a kaleidoscope of jeweled colors twist in my head as I take a celebratory swig of jungle juice from my plastic red cup, belting out lyrics like there's no tomorrow. One of these days, if I drink enough, maybe there won't be. A tomorrow. I haven't decided yet how much I want one.

At the least I'd like to not dread waking up every day.

We follow with "Dream On" by Aerosmith, "Bed of Roses" by Bon Jovi, and I'm launching into one of my favorites, Janice Joplin, when the cops roll up. Damn.

Lights flash and sirens bloop, and just like that, someone cuts the sound.

Just when I was thinking guitar boy might be worth going home and fooling around with a little, he mumbles some nonsense about how he can't afford to get caught and runs off with his guitar case slung on his back. Oh well.

A blurry picture forms in my soggy brain; he's got something other than guitar picks and an instrument in that case. Now I'm not sure if I'm extra sorry I didn't go home with him or glad I didn't. If he gets caught, then the latter. I don't love jail. My mother's always such a nightmare about these things.

A pretty blonde who stopped by our group earlier climbs up onto the stage. "Hey. Kate, right?" She leans in to whisper in my ear. "You still want those pills? I've got them."

"You bet I do." Oh. Score. In my drunken haze, I forgot I'd asked, but yes. Definitely. So much yes. My doctor warned me on my last visit that he was refilling my Percocet and valium for the final time.

It's been a long road. Too log. I'm not ready to be without my pain meds.

She backs down to the shadowy edge off the side of the stage. "Over here so nobody can see. The bottle's in my back pocket. You can swap it with the money."

The police are making their way through the crowd but they're still way up near the entrance. It'll be tight, getting the pills from her and hiding them. So I move in, sliding my hand around her waist like we're about to have a drunken make-out sesh.

Someone grabs my arm. "Sweetheart, I really wouldn't. That girl's probably a narc and you're way too pretty for jail."

"What the hell?" Even though I haven't heard it in forever, the cocky tone of my old friend spins me around. "Alonzo? Holy shit, what are you doing here? I haven't seen you since…"

Since shortly after our friend Terrence's funeral. I couldn't go since I was still in the hospital. Which everyone made a point of telling me was *so lucky*. After all, it was better than what had happened to Terrence.

Lucky. That's not the word I'd use.

He reaches forward to hug me, but then I notice who he's got standing behind him. Laying eyes on the muscular build and easy movement of the guy hovering over Alonzo's shoulder freezes me from head to toe, even as my racing heart tries to make a break for the trees. Sharp eyes I've looked into a thousand times find mine in spite of the darkness. Eyes that can smile on their own or dress you down with the subtle arch of one dark eyebrow the way they're doing right now.

Ty. Oh God.

I really think I might pass out. "What are you doing here?" I turn to Alonzo. *The traitor.* "What's he doing here?"

Never mind that Alonzo surely must have brought Ty with him. What are either of them doing here?

For years, my world revolved around Tyler Thacker. I would have followed him off the end of the earth. Like a lost puppy, I looked to him for everything: companionship, protection, and even love.

Before the accident, he'd finally found the success he deserved. His MMA career took off, making him too big for the little town we'd lived in. Maybe also too big for me.

After the accident, he disappeared. I haven't seen him in almost two years. Not sure how I feel seeing him now. Mentally, anyway. Physically, I'm flushed with an excitement I shouldn't feel. I step forward before I stop myself, something deep inside my muscles driving me toward what was once so familiar.

Even standing in the shadowy tree line as he is now, even damaged as my head is, I'd know him anywhere. Glow sticks and lighters from milling partygoers burnish his dark brown skin, his usually smiling face now solemn with his chin held high.

In the time that I've had to recover I've stared at dozens and dozens of pictures to try and reboot my memory. More of them of Tyler than I'd care to admit. Seeing him in person? It's not even remotely the same.

God. Those full lips and high cheekbones of his might look better with the easygoing smile he used to wear, but there's no denying that his face makes my stomach kind of fluttery all the same. I choose to blame that feeling on the drinks and not goofball sentimentality.

Kinda wish he'd smile now, but there's none in sight.

Guess I don't blame him, considering how we left things. Or didn't. Either way I'm still finding it hard to breathe. Ty's abrupt departure from my life may have hurt, but seeing him still makes my chest do funny things.

I've run my fingers over every inch of that face, of skin that glowed warm in the sun when he'd walk me home in the summer afternoons. I've kissed the corners of those bottomless eyes and his full mouth and proud nose until he wouldn't let me anymore. The muscular arms and shoulders I caressed with my hands… Those are bigger, I think. I hate that my palms prickle with an urge to know if I'm right.

Lately my memories of Ty have lain buried in the murky recesses of my brain, like they're drowning underwater and impossible to reach. Visible, but barely. Now those velvety lips are vivid. The feel of them on my ear, my cheek, and my own mouth roar to life in a place I'd thought the car accident had destroyed.

Police cut the power and blackness falls with a bang. Lighters wink out around us here and there. The only significant illumination in this defunct RV park now is from flashing red and blue lights or those industrial-powered police flashlights. Still. As the lights swing, I can see the broad span of Ty's shoulders and a vague suggestion of how his chest and arms bulge under his sweatshirt.

He was always so big. Even bigger now than when I last saw him, if such a thing is possible. Bigger than when I last touched him. The longer I look the more certain I am.

People stream past us. Cops herding everyone towards the exit. The supposed narc with my pills has vanished. One of my fellow partygoers thumps me from behind, sending my body and brain spinning. Spinning right into Ty.

I land with a rough "oof" and find my hands planted on his chest. Oh, yes. He's definitely bigger than before.

In my defense, he's a full six feet tall and I'm five-four. His pecs are pretty much *right there*. Whatever ugly history is between us, there's no denying he's always been handsome.

"Uh. Awkward. Sorry." Trying to push away somehow only gets us closer. Our legs and feet tangle. "Hey, are all the trees and stuff spinning or are we the ones turning in circles?"

Ty squints down at me. "You're only drunk, right? You didn't take any of those pills tonight?"

I bat away the fingers, trying to pry my eyes open. Checking my pupils, I'm sure. "No, *Mom*. Thanks for asking."

He grabs my hand and pulls me toward the exit. "Good. That's what the police will be checking for. Now let's get out of here."

I stumble behind him. Part of me wants to get stubborn and dig in my heels, because of reasons. Because it's Tyler and we have a lot that should be resolved before we go anywhere holding hands again. Because I don't let anyone lead me *anywhere*, and he and Alonzo still haven't explained what in the name of good music or bad liquor they're doing here.

Cops are stopping people on their way out though. The quicker we all get through the gates, the better.

"Where's your shirt?" Ty gives me a judgy look over his shoulder.

"Dunno. Alonzo, I hope you have a car. Pretty sure it's a long trek home."

"To your place? Eight miles, I believe. To mine, where we're eventually going? Yeah, a lot longer. But since I'm not stupid enough to cross state lines with a drunk girl whose family might decide to report you missing, we're going to take you back to your place first."

I stop.

Ty tugs my arm again.

I yank my hand out of his. "Okay, no. Pass. Whatever this is about? Definitely one thousand percent pass. You said nothing about a road trip or talking to my mom."

Alonzo turns to me and puts his hands on his hips. A breeze comes though and makes me shiver. Now that I'm neither drinking nor sweating up on a stage, the fact that I've been dumb enough to toss my shirt is biting me in the ass. Most of my decisions do.

"For the love of—Put this on." Ty rips off his hoodie and then tosses it to me.

"Thanks." That's as far as I'll go toward admitting out loud that I'm cold.

"Man, what are you even doing out here? Trying to make yourself sick?"

Maybe. I don't know. "Since when did you care? I haven't heard from you in almost two years, and suddenly you show up to rescue me like some sort of knight in shining sweatpants?"

"There a problem here, kids?"

Kid. Ty and Alonzo are twenty-four. I'm almost twenty-one. Try telling that to my mother though, who took away my car keys and my college fund so I had no choice but to stick close to home after the accident. Or Officer Friendly here, who's shining a flashlight in my face so bright I'm biting down hard on the urge to do a vampire hiss in his face.

Alonzo steps forward. "No trouble, officer. My sister here had too much to drink. I'll be sure to get her home safe."

The officer shines his light in my face for probably a few more seconds. Feels like forever. Then he aims his authority and sunshiny brightness at Alonzo and Ty. "You been drinking tonight? Any drugs I should know about?"

"No, sir," they say in unison. Alonzo tips his head. "She has. Been drinking, that is. Like I said. She's legal though. And I'm driving."

I'm not legal. My ID is at home. I'm banking on the cop being too busy to check.

He looks at us all a beat longer before he points down the messy field of parked cars with his flashlight. "Get out of here. Be careful."

"Absolutely, officer. Have a nice night." Boy Scout Tyler disappears once we're alone again, grabbing my arm and pulling me towards the exit. "Man. Let's get out of here."

Alonzo grumbles and stalks ahead of us. "Lucky thing that dude's got bigger problems tonight."

Yeah. Alonzo and I don't look like siblings. At all.

"Alonzo, seriously. You could've texted first. What are you doing here? Did someone die? And I do not want to go back home. Not now. My mom might still be up and she'll know where I went if I don't sneak in late enough."

Ty, who's still holding my arm, gives it a squeeze. "Nobody's dead. Alonzo said you've been ignoring his messages so we came in person to keep your ass from ODing or getting swept up in a raid."

I haven't been ignoring so much as... Okay, I've been ignoring him. "You guys, I don't need a babysitter."

Neither of them answer. Everyone trudges ahead, stone-faced, until we're through the hastily set-up police perimeter guarding the opening. Everyone gets a friendly pat-down and a video camera in their face before they're allowed to leave.

Me, I make my best effort at standing upright for the good officers. Frankly, I think I deserve an award. It's not the alcohol so much as shock. Ty's here.

Ty's here.

So many pictures and memories. Sometimes if I didn't know better I'd think I dreamed him.

Both guys are walking ahead of me now, striding on much longer legs that leave me weaving and wobbling to catch up. Well, fine. "Hey. I didn't ask you to come here and track me down. I can find another ride."

No idea where the guys I arrived with went to, but it's not usually hard to find someone who will give me a lift. Especially not if I remove Ty's hoodie.

"No." All of a sudden Alonzo turns to face me. "You're going to come with us. You're going to do this, because you fucking owe us, Kate. We made each other a promise and you have not held up your end."

Shit. Alonzo's bringing out the big guilt guns. And like that, I'm not nearly drunk enough anymore.

#

Ty - then

The night I met Kate, I walked her home.

The town of Aspiration, South Carolina, was dying. Tons of little communities that had sprung up because of the railroads or the factories or whatever, all losing hope as the schools, grocery stores, and other businesses peeled whitewash and tried to pretend everything was fine.

Hell. Even the grass had given up in Aspiration. The world around us faded to a sad, dead greenish-brown on the ground.

So some of seniors from the high school, we'd taken up fighting in the lot of what used to be a pretty damn good restaurant, the Suzy-Q. Sandwiches you could barely get your mouth around. Don't get me started on the fried chicken and garlic knots. I'd missed my gran, and the chicken was almost as good as hers. Waitress there used to serve me for free if I gave her a good smile. Sad day when that place closed.

Still, money could be made grappling in that gravel lot where people had once parked their trucks for Saturday night dinners. All you had to do was be the guy who didn't go down. Easy cash when you were big like me, especially when word traveled and guys came from neighboring towns in the name of a challenge.

One night, there she was in the crowd. Couldn't have looked more lost in that long-long skirt and button-up blouse she had on. The innocent look of that braided hair didn't help. Even covered up as she was, too many guys on the lot looked at her like they were at their last meal and she'd just delivered a case of Tastykakes.

I'd herded her out of there before any of them slobbering bags of testosterone could get too close. "What's a nice-looking girl like you doing watching guys beat each other bloody?"

"Actually, I recognized you from school. You're a senior, right? I saw you guys on my way home from the library. Marisol, at the front desk, she lets me stay late sometimes. My parents are… Well. Anyway. You're really good. I think. Not that I'm any kind of expert on the fine art of guys knocking each other senseless."

I had to turn away so she wouldn't see the pride on my face. "School, huh? You also a senior?"

"Umm… Not exactly. I'll be sixteen in May."

Danger! Danger!

I stopped on the corner and put up my hand to block her face from my line of sight. That fluttery, grateful smile of hers? I'd seen it from enough girls. No lie, I'd taken advantage of it a time or two. I couldn't cave to its power right now.

"Okay, then. You are officially too young for me even to look at you, never mind standing this close."

That made her laugh. Yeah, but I was serious though. I'd turned eighteen the month before and aged out of foster care. My major priorities were buying food and finishing school. Throwing a little something to the friends who let me crash in their spaces. Spending time with an underage white girl? That fell under the category of "Complications I Won't Even Pretend to Have Time For."

"So, do you do that a lot? The fighting?" She rolled on as if I hadn't told her I couldn't be around her anymore.

And because even quiet towns like Aspiration had their bad elements, I kept on walking beside her when she started going again. Who knew what else was out there this time of evening?

"As often as I can. I'm good at it. Helps me let off steam. Gives me something to control when things feel out of control."

I scratched at the back of my neck, unused to oversharing. Uncertain why I was doing it then. "It's also a good way to make money without getting into dealing. Which I promised my grandmother I'd never do."

"That's sweet. Your promise to your grandmother."

"She was a good woman. Died when my brother and I were finishing middle school."

"I'm sorry." For a second, her hand rested on my arm. "At least you have good feelings about her. My grandmother cooks all of her food in ten pounds of butter and then pinches my arm fat and tells me I'm looking heavy. That's my mom's mom. My dad's mom died before I was born."

We walked past what had once been a small strip of stores. Out of a bookstore, barber, bakery, and pet store, only the barber shop remained open. I put my distance between me and her as we walked past what was still a town gossip mill.

"I don't think you need to worry about anyone who tries to make you feel like you're not pretty enough." Even under all those clothes and a hazy, charcoal sky I could see she had a petite body with curves in the right places, whether seeing them was smart or not.

When she got all quiet and glanced up before looking away, I realized what I'd done. Damn. First I'd gone and told her I couldn't look at her, and then I'd made it clear exactly how closely I had looked.

Excellent work, Thacker.

"Well. I'm right up there. With the ugly pea-green paint and the light-up flamingo on the lawn." She pointed down Jay Street to a row of neat but aging houses lined up on one of the few roads that still looked like part of an actual neighborhood.

Her house had lights on inside and a television going. This definitely didn't feel like a meet-the-parents moment. "I'll say goodbye here," I said. "No more staying late at the library. No more hanging out in the crowd at street fights. You got me?"

"Hey, you walked me all the way home, but you didn't tell me your name."

No harm in telling her, right? She could easily find out at school. "Tyler."

"Can I call you Ty?"

"You don't need to call me anything, because I'm not going to see you around those fights anymore."

"I'll see you at school," she said. Then she planted a kiss on my cheek, which was more endearing than I wanted it to be. The differences in our height made her have to hop a little to reach me. "Thanks, Ty."

"Hey. No more walking home late."

She smiled and ran off with her backpack in her hands. Wasn't 'til later I realized she'd never agreed to my directive about not showing up at the fights. And she did show up again. And again.

And again.

2. FIERY DISASTERS

Kate

"So what's going on?"

Okay. Back when I was still in high school and Ty's career was about to take off, we did one of those crazy we'll-always-look-out-for-each-other pacts. All four of us, before our little group scattered and our lives went in different directions. Before Terrence decided he hated me.

Who believes that stuff, right? At the time, being younger and more starry-eyed than the rest of the gang, I did kinda believe. It feels now like it all happened in another life. Ty and I lost touch. Alonzo and I promised to stay in touch, but only do so through overblown social media updates.

Every day is the same cycle. Pain, helplessness, and regret. Lather, rinse, repeat. Getting through the day is hard enough without bothering about being socially appropriate on the Internet.

I want to tell them so. Really though, it's been a nightmare lately at home. Dad's gone. Mom is… *Seething* is a good word. We're both seething. She's pissed because my insistence on a pesky thing like medical treatment got her in trouble with her church. I'm pissed because of the thing she's pissed about.

Mostly we avoid fighting by me not coming home until after she's in bed. Much like I'd planned on doing tonight.

We're standing outside the exit while cracked-out party people try to head home. The guys are both staring me down, wearing coordinating expressions of frustration and impatience, not answering. In the light of a pair of bright headlamps, Ty's intense glare does funny things to my stomach. Or it could be the alcohol. Not sure when I last ate.

I wave my proverbial white flag. "Seriously, you guys have me worried. What did you need that was so insanely important you had to drive all this way?"

Alonzo relaxes his tight posture. Less Fred, more Shaggy. "One of our roommates plays bass in a band. Indy rock, mostly. You'll definitely like their stuff."

Is this really the big emergency? "How do you know what music I listen to?"

"You post videos online all the time. 'Got this stuck in my head and misery loves company.' You think we don't all know that's code for 'I love this so much I play it on repeat but I'm afraid to admit it and lose my cool points?' Yeah. So, Layla's band lost their lead singer. They have a good following. You need to get out of Aspiration and do something with yourself. Win-win, right?"

Okay, wait… I look at Ty. "You guys want me to sing in a band. And you drove all the way here to track me down at a party in the middle of the night?"

Ty lifts his shoulder. "We tried leaving earlier, but first we had to get our hands on a car."

Am I more wasted than I thought? Am I passed out under a tree somewhere and this is all a fucked-up dream? "You guys can't be serious."

Alonzo gives me a "Search me" shrug and walks toward the cars again. "We should stop and eat. Grab some pancakes to soak up all that alcohol so you don't puke in my roommate's car."

Something nudges at me. This is all too weird. I close my eyes, but all I see are bright balls of blurry light. "Come on, Alonzo. What's the deal?"

"The deal is I said I knew the best singer, and I promised her I'd get you down there. I keep my promises, Kate. Like how I promised I'd look out for you, and you're one red party cup and some muscle relaxers away from being face down in a ditch. Or being a badass bitch's girlfriend."

Ouch. "Excuse me, but I would be the badass bitch in that scenario. Whatever. This is in no way a good idea, but fine. I'll come with you for pancakes. Even though this is a fiery disaster waiting to happen."

If there's one thing I know, it's fiery disasters.

He slugs me in the arm. "I knew you'd see it our way."

"Don't say 'our,' I'm just along for the ride," Ty says.

Alonzo ignores him. "You're gonna be surprised. You'll see. You both will," he says.

Surprised. Yeah. That's what I'm afraid of. Whatever the crazy reason they're here, we did once make each other a promise. "Hey, someone better deliver on the pancakes."

#

Ty

I keep wondering how a person's supposed to keep going when they've lost both halves of their heart.

Nah. Strike *that* right there.

When you've had half your heart—the half that was your perfect mirror, the half that was so essential you figured anything else in your world could collapse but with that one piece of you still beating, you'd be okay—

that half? When that half gets ripped out so fast your head whips back from the blow. Then, just when you think you can try to stand, the rest that was trying its damndest to keep going gets yanked out and crushed.

Then dusted over the hospital food of the girl you loved, and eaten with her gelatinous, green dessert.

Letting Alonzo talk me into this trip was straight-up insane. I tell myself so even as I follow him and Kate back to his roommate's car.

Seeing her again kicked me harder than I expected. I'm fighting to stand in front of her without doubling over from the blow. It's almost like she's fishing around inside my chest cavity to see if there might be any missing pieces she left behind.

Probably so she can step on them with those fine-assed boots she's wearing. Not as if she's wearing a hell of a lot else.

It might piss me off, knowing so many people tonight have looked at her in nothing but a sports bra, but there's too much pain in my chest to feel anything else. Hurt nobody gets to see, because it's mine alone.

So I'll do what I've always done, and smile. Pretend it's good to see her. Pretend it's like old times, even though those times are buried in the ground with my heart. With my brother.

Except I can't pretend. "So, what is all this craziness, Kate? You're the hard-partying kind now?" I try to ask with my usual easy humor, but there's an edge cutting underneath. Part of me wants her to hear, because I want an answer to my real questions.

What is wrong with you? You died and came back, and this is what you do with your second chance at life?

"It works. I get to dance. Sometimes I get to sing." She shrugs and tucks her short, dark hair behind one ear. Like she cares less than not at all. For all I know, she doesn't. The girl I knew wore what her mother told her to and cried if she got an A-*minus* on a test.

This girl is not the Kate I knew. Except for a few scars, her face and body look the same. But I worry her soul is in the ground next to my brother.

"What, you don't like it?" She doesn't look at me when she talks but that's easier. It's hard to look her in the face. Her brown eyes and her full lips look exactly to me like they always did, even gunked-up with that cat-eye whateveryoucallit and a million tons of mascara.

Her lips may be redder, but my gut tells me they're still the softest lips I ever kissed. The ones I can't erase no matter how many came before or after.

I was her first kiss. Her first everything. I met an innocent girl on her way home from the library, and now I'm looking at… Man, I don't even know.

"Alonzo showed me your Instagram feed," I say instead of answering her question. "You've been up to all kinds of things."

She snaps her fingers. "I knew it had to be the Instagram pictures. That's how you guys found me, right? I posted a picture of the party flier."

"You got lucky. Alonzo says the promotor throwing this thing has a history of getting busted by police."

"Hmm. I get it."

I don't say a thing. She always did like to try to read my mind when I was in a quiet mood. Sometimes a guy wants to think his thoughts. That so bad?

Only person who left me alone about what I was thinking was Terrence. He had his own quiet moods. We understood that about each other. Hindsight being what it is, I think I really ought to have asked more questions about what was on his mind during those moments.

Another few paces and I can't take the volume of her silent righteousness. "I can hear you thinking we're wrong all the way over there."

She seems to find that funny. "You always did think you knew me."

Funny. "I was thinking the same thing about you."

Alonzo spins to face us. "Kids. Don't make me turn this rave around." He cuts his side-eye to the cops coming in our direction from where the party had been going on.

I rub the back of my neck with a hard breath and speed up, grabbing Kate's arm on my way past. When she opens her mouth on a "Hey" to protest my hand on her, I put another arm around her shoulder to pull her close. Like we're a couple. Like old times.

"How about we all get out of here peacefully, okay? I don't want trouble with the police. Neither do you, based on how you're still not quite walking in a straight line. We wind up getting stopped, it's gonna be a bad night for everyone."

She clamps her mouth shut.

"Yeah, that's what I thought."

"Man. I'm starving, people." Up ahead of us, Alonzo rubs a shameless hand over his belly. "Don't know about you all, but I would commit murder for some pigs in a blanket right about now. Oheythereofficer."

Dumbass mock salutes a passing uniform. Lucky for us, the dude only blasts us in the face with a sunlight-bright flashlight and keeps on walking. Whatever it is they're here to find, we don't have any.

I look down at Kate. *Hopefully* we don't have any.

"You clean, Kate?" I hate the idea of this girl taking some kind of illegal pills. Makes the back of my throat burn. Knowing the pain she's carried and the role I played in thrusting it upon her, I don't ask all the questions I'm dying to.

Her dark chocolate eyes glitter under a streetlight when she glares up at me. "Define clean, Ty. I rode with three twenty-something guys on the way here, and one of them spilled party punch on me. I could maybe use a shower."

A low growl pushes out of my throat, but I don't take her bait. She knows damn well this isn't about whether or not she needs a shower, and I know the state she's worked herself into means she wants to be contrary for contrary's sake.

So instead I take my frustration out on the easiest target. I lean forward and slap a hand on Alonzo's shoulder. "And what is up with you, dumbass? You trying to get us arrested?"

"Hey, you know I have a hard-on for that command presence shit. The uniform, the badge, the gun…" He ups the ick factor by adding a dramatic shiver. "Bonus points for those badass motorcycle boots."

Alonzo makes my head hurt. "Fool."

My friend is grinning. No cares in the world. He turns himself backward to talk to us while he walks, which strikes me as a stupid move considering the number of passed-out party kids we've walked by on our way already.

"You're going to trip over somebody." Whatever. I love Alonzo practically like a brother, but he's on my list of people who will someday die doing something ridiculous. It won't be a car crash or a heart attack. It'll be cuz he walked off a cliff while reading on his iPhone or he propositioned a member of a gun-running biker gang cuz "the dude's tats looked crazy hot."

"Yeah, we'll see who's the dumbass when I get us out of a ticket on the way home by using my manly wiles."

As my gran would have said, *lawd bless the poor child*. "How about we just don't get stopped?"

Alonzo shows me the back of his hand. "Your plans are never fun."

We reach the mouth of the park where the "party" was being held. Soon as we're past the police barriers, Kate pulls away. Fine.

"Don't worry, baby. Got my cooties shot."

She crosses her eyes at me and sticks out her tongue.

Hell. "Well as long as we're being mature and everything."

When I met Kate, she was on the honor roll. First chair soprano in the choir, Juliet in the school play, and class treasurer. The fact that I was about to graduate aside, I knew she was so out of my league I shouldn't try to look at her with a planetarium microscope.

Now? She's half naked and displaying the emotional maturity of a toddler who got her toys taken away. It's enough to break my brain.

"I'll be mature when I get my pancakes." She shrugs. "Or I'll drunk dial my mom and tell her you and Alonzo kidnapped me. Fifty-fifty. Anyway, you're the one who mentioned cooties."

Cheese and damn fried rice.

"Tell your mother that and I'll kill us all in a murder-suicide to save her the trouble of skinning me alive."

She shrugs, as if this is something we discuss every day. As if it hasn't been two years since we've so much as talked. "I died once. It was no big."

I stop. With my jaw clenched, I growl, "No big? Is that a joke?" Because to me it was big. It was awfully. Damn. Big.

"Okay, okay. Guys." We pile into the car and Alonzo pulls us out onto the highway. Heading I'm not sure where. He seems to know. "When did we graduate from midnight breakfast to murder-suicide? Can't we just get some of those cool pancakes where they make the happy face out of whipped cream and chocolate chips? I could sure as hell use a happy face pancake right about now."

Sure looks that way. Alonzo's chill about almost everything but he hates to drive. Right now tension is thick in his voice even while he makes jokes.

I turn to look at Kate where she's sprawled in the backseat, half-lidded and pouty. I'm irritated that my basic maleness still responds to everything feminine about her. She may be in rough shape, but that only reminds me of how she used to be. How *we* used to be.

How I wasn't there to protect her when I should have been. Maybe if I had been, she wouldn't be like this now.

Which is, all of Alonzo's BS aside, really why I'm here. It's been a long time since my world crashed and burned. If I knew Kate'd gone on to live a good life, I could handle letting her go, but that's not what it's been. I've seen her social media feeds. Heard updates via late, drunken texts she sends to Alonzo. She's about to crash and burn, too.

I wasn't there to pull her out of the wreckage before. I'm here now.

When I look back again, she's staring out the window. Hair swept back from her face, lips parted, eyes wide. If I had to guess, I'd almost say she looks scared. The thought jerks hard at the center of my chest.

Huh. Maybe there's a chance I've still got something beating in there after all. I wonder if it's enough.

3. KEEP IT IN YOUR PANTS

Kate

"Oh. My. God. These are the best pancakes ever."

When you've been out in the chill and you're still nursing a wrecked party buzz, there's just something about a fluffy stack of warm, buttery (did I mention fluffy? Sooo fluffy) goodness that makes you want to fall face-first on it and attack it like a starving pack of zombies.

Maybe I've watched too much of *The Walking Dead*, but I stand by my point. The rest of Carolina can keep their fish fries. Late-night fluffy pancakes for comfort? Win.

Sitting across from your sort of ex-boyfriend while he *not* sort of scowls at you with disapproval? Not winning at all. Decidedly un-win. What am I doing here again?

Ohyeah. Pancakes. Also, I made a ridiculous promise ages ago.

I point at the stack in front of Ty's crossed arms. "Do you plan on eating those? Because I'd hate to see them go to waste, and if you sit there grinding your teeth like that, you won't be able to chew."

He turns to Alonzo. "This was a bad idea."

"You could have stayed home," Alonzo says.

I kick one of them under the table as I dump syrup on my pancake. "So, you guys drove all the way up here just to drag me away from a party. I'm touched. Tell me more about this band thing."

They glance at each other. Alonzo says, "Hey, pass me the syrup, would you?"

Okay. I may not remember how many drinks I've had tonight. I may not remember where I left my shirt. I may not even be sure whether my vision is still crossed or if it's that godawful carpet they've got in this waffle house, or possibly I lost a contact lens during all the confusion tonight…

I do know that *pass me the syrup* is no answer to my question.

So I stick my tongue out at the both of them in answer to their nonanswer. "You know what? You guys can just drop me off at home and go back to whatever it is you both spend your bro-time doing. If you can't at least be honest with me, then what's the point?"

Alonzo hands back the syrup. "All right. So my friend Layla. She's the bassist. The other two band members are Travis and Bree. Trav is our guitar player and Bree plays drums. They're a talented bunch and the music is great. I think you'll love 'em."

A few bites of pancake and my stomach is settling. God bless late-night diners. "So if they're all kinds of awesome, why'd the lead singer bail when they were about to make it big?"

"The call came after she moved out."

"Still. Why?"

Alonzo puts his fork down quietly and looks away. A glance over at his friend and back down at his food, and then Ty's eyes light up.

"What?" I'm looking back and forth from one to the other. Alonzo, usually so chatty, is now a vault. Ty is nodding his head as if his favorite Leon Bridges song is playing, and not the twangy, old-style country our waffle house is playing over the loudspeaker.

"Alonzo slept with her. He literally screwed his roommate's band out of a lead singer," Ty murmurs with amusement glowing on his face.

That pulls up my drooping head. "Was this somehow intentional?"

Ty flicks Alonzo's arm. "Nah, Alonzo's got this sweet setup. His house is right on the edge of Evergreen Grove, which is tiny like Aspiration, but not dead yet. It's all picturesque and whatnot. It's also *right* next to a college town full of all the action he can grab. Except he also got greedy and grabbed one of his roommates. So she moved out the next day, which is how come he's desperately begging you to bail him out."

If my jaw dropped any lower, I'd be licking pancake syrup off my plate. Alonzo was like the puppy dog of our group at one time. Faithfully following his buddies Ty and Terrence everywhere. Even more than me. I never saw him with girlfriends or boyfriends. And now he's apparently screwing his way through an entire college campus? I guess we've all changed.

I stare across the table at Ty. In spite of the holes the accident made in my memory, the way his smile dimples his cheeks and his dark eyes sparkle, he looks exactly the same. So maybe we haven't *all* changed.

Back to Alonzo. "I'm sure the phrase 'keep it in your pants' has crossed your radar once or twice? It seems apropos for not fucking around with your roommates." Honestly, it's none of my business who Alonzo gets it on with. I've had my share of stupid experiences in the name of forgetting my troubles.

What bugs me is that at first I thought Alonzo came to find me because he was looking out for an old friend. Now it sounds more like he needed to save his own ass and thought reliable old Kate would be there to bail him out.

Except reliable old Kate died off the side of a desolate stretch of Route 27. With a pin in my wrist, a broken arm and leg, two cracked vertebrae, and a rebuilt orbital bone, I'm now Damaged Kate. Damaged Kate has subzero fucks to give.

"You know what? You guys can go ahead and take me home. I'm not here to save anyone's bacon. I'm not even good at saving my own."

A half-sober angel on my shoulder pipes up and warns me that I'm sabotaging myself. Alonzo was right. I've been looking for a reason to get out of Aspiration. A band to sing with would be nice. The little one a few towns over that I sang with before my accident, well, they all moved on. After my injury, it was no longer a good fit. The up-tempo jazzy stuff they wanted to perform no longer tasted right on my tongue.

My brain had changed. All the alto sax and crashing symbols were too bright in my head.

I do miss being part of a band. But I want to be wanted for *me*. Not because Alonzo screwed the pooch. Or the lead singer, anyway.

Alonzo reaches across the table, nearly dragging his sleeve through syrup. Lovely. "Kate, please. I'm—"

"Nah." Ty puts a hand on Alonzo's arm, bringing his sleeve back out of harm's way. "You don't need to beg. We don't need to put a gun at her back."

Those eyes. Dark. Endless. So serious right now. And God, why do guys always get the good eyelashes?

I'd say I like it better when he smiles, but I still can't find it in myself to look away.

"You want to go home, we'll take you home."

Actually, I'm sort of on the fence. Part of me wants to see what this band thing is about. I've bummed around the house for the past couple of years, doing nothing but PT and doctors' appointments until I can't take it anymore.

My mom and I can't stand each other. My parents split because of the accident. Dad moved away to find a better job. Can't blame him.

I'm not really able to work. The mere thought of school makes me anxious, though I've wanted to re-apply to colleges about a thousand times. My pre-accident plan was to major in business and I don't even know why.

I can't drive. I'm barely able to buy my own groceries.

My entire life is a cycle of *before* and *wait, what was I supposed to be doing?* Until I realize the answer is nothing because nobody expects anything from me anymore.

I'm stuck. In a loop of my own making.

So no, I don't want to go home. To where my mother and I fight while she watches me the way a CO watches prison inmates. (No lie, there's a mannequin in my bed right now. That's how ridic this entire thing is.)

But I've stomped my foot and complained, so... "Yes. Take me home." Even if I wanted to go with them, I need to pick up a few things. I can't leave wearing nothing but cargo pants and a sports bra.

Ty throws some cash on the table and jumps up. "You heard her, man. Let's head out."

We climb in the back of the sweet-assed vintage mustang Alonzo borrowed from his roommate. Earlier I was too hammered to notice, but it's a great car. The kind I'd want to have if I was able to drive again.

No need to direct them to my house. Ty once walked me home practically every night of the week.

"Just stop right here." I direct them to cut the engine at the end of the road. Same place Ty used to leave me because he was worried my parents would freak if they saw us together.

"What are we dropping you off all the way up here for?"

Ty groans from the passenger seat. "Wake your ass up, Alonzo." He looks back at me. It's not the first time he's made eye contact since the party but it's the first time I don't feel like he's trying to analyze me. "Her parents were always protective."

"Some things get even better with age." I find myself smiling at him. Letting the fog of my memory cloud over his last words to me, said in the hospital when he thought I was out in la-la land.

Unbelievably, he's smiling too. Maybe he's also forgotten he told me it was my fault Terrence was dead. He must have, to be able to give me that kind of smile.

Sadly, I can't forget. I taste carob in my mouth every time I remember. Fake chocolate substitute makes me want to vomit, and so does the guy I used to love more than my own existence telling me I killed his twin brother.

"Well, thanks for the ride, guys."

I push my way out into the night. It's chilly, but tolerable. One thing you can say for the south, even in winter the cold isn't awful. As I near the northeast corner of my house, I realize it's tolerable because I still have Ty's sweatshirt. I should return it, but I'm not going back now.

Except the front door opens, and out storms my mother. In the track pants and cat shirt that are her nightclothes, with torn socks on her feet, because God forbid she stop tithing long enough to have money for new clothing.

She works for the church as an office administrator. Pretty sure all we do is give the paycheck right back after she receives it each month.

"I found that thing in your bed. I don't have to tell you how much trouble you're in. I almost called the police."

"Mom. I'm twenty-one in two months. The police aren't going to care that I stayed out late."

She slaps the doorframe with ineffectual anger. "You live under my roof, young lady. You follow my rules. You're lucky I don't blister your hide."

Ugh. Seriously. I'm so, so everloving tired of this. "If we followed your rules I'd be dead now, Mom. Definitely you missed your window on being able to spank me by about fifteen years."

She draws her hand back. It looks like this might be the time she finally loses her patience and cracks me one, but no. She does stick a stern finger in my face. "You. Have no faith. No gratitude. No—"

"I know, Mom. My desire to bow down to your mandates got wiped out when I took a delivery truck to the head. So right now I'm gonna go, and I'll let you know when I change my mind about the faith healings, 'kay?"

I duck under her arm and hook left into my bedroom to grab a backpack from my closet. It's full of clothes, cash, and a few important personal items. For months it's sat in there while I watched *Lost* and *Grey's Anatomy* one season at a time and told myself maybe I'd finally go somewhere other than my bedroom. After I snag it, sticking a hand inside to be sure my notebook and cash are still in there, I spin on my heel and turn back for the door. On my way out, I swipe my never-used license from my dresser.

Maybe Ty and Alonzo are still outside, maybe not. I don't care. Them showing up reminded me how much I hate this rut I've been in, and I'll limp three towns over to the bus station if I have to.

Two things I have going for me: my dad helped me open my own bank account when he and Mom started divorce proceedings, and despite Ty thinking the accident was somehow my fault, the poor schlub driving the truck that hit us the day of the accident had amphetamines in his system. The settlement money I got from the shipping company was decent, and I haven't touched it much. Unlike the college fund, which was controlled by my parents, Mom hasn't been able to get her mitts on my settlement to hand it all over to her cult-y worship leader.

A flash of headlights from up the block tells me Alonzo and Ty are still there. They waited. I try not to like the rush of relief I feel quite so much. This past couple of years has taught me not to lean on anyone. More than likely, people let you down.

All the same, I'm glad not to have to walk. My body still doesn't handle endurance stuff too well. I throw a smile at Alonzo when I climb back in. "Hey. Thanks for waiting."

Ty's propped his forehead on his fist, as if he's sleeping. He isn't, but I guess he's no longer interested in talking.

"So." Alonzo looks around as he flips a U-turn on my parents' road. "Glad you decided to join us. Hotel?"

Nobody answers. I'm looking at Tyler and he's not saying a word. I'm wondering if it's me or did something happen after I left the car?

"Great idea." Alonzo nods, agreeing with himself. "It's late. We'll all feel better after a good night's sleep. Hotel room it is."

"Sure. Yeah. Sounds good," I murmur. Because, really, I'm still wondering what's going on with Ty, and also wondering why I care. He's the one who left and never came back.

Which makes me wonder again... What is he even doing here?

Bigger question: What in the hell am I going to do next? Sneaking in failed miserably, and I've just all but given my mom the finger and torched her house as I walked out the door.

"Hotel sounds good," I say again to nobody in particular as I close my eyes and lean against the window. My head is still sort of fuzzy. Maybe everything will seem better after I sleep. This Evergreen Grove place we're going to might not even suck.

#

Ty

"She's passed out back there."

I look in the rearview to confirm Alonzo's comment. "Yeah, well. Seemed like she had a lot to drink tonight. Who knows what else."

He shakes his head. "Didn't look to me like she was on anything else. Not to mention if she'd done anything extracurricular, she probably wouldn't be sleeping. Bet she's just exhausted."

Leave it to Alonzo to know his party drugs. "So how come you're here babysitting her instead of back home getting baked like every other night of the week?"

He holds up a finger. "Not every night, for one thing. For another, you know why. I've been trying to get her out of that house for months now. This singing gig is an excuse. Not that getting Layla off my ass isn't gravy. Anyway, if I'd sent you by yourself, you two probably would've killed each other."

"Man, I've never even strangled *you* when you deserved it. Pretty sure I can handle keeping the peace with Kate." Though I can't deny we have some unfinished business. I look out the window to avoid saying more. "I see lightning. We oughta find a place to crash before the sky opens."

"Right. Anyway." He knocks his knuckles on the window. "What happened to Terrence pushed us all apart. She's still family. Some things you do for family." He glances over his shoulder before slowing down for a U-turn.

Come to find out, there's a decent-looking place with a restaurant and a gas station next door. I hadn't noticed at first because I was busy avoiding Alonzo's curious looks. And his comments.

Family's a thing I thought I'd lost a long time ago. But Alonzo, he was in the system way longer than me and my brother. I guess for him, family is a thing of your own making. He's tried to keep us close, even when we were far away.

I'm silent while he pulls into a space near the hotel's lit carport. My body though, it's answered even if I haven't. My chest is tight and my heart can't find its rhythm. This conversation's messing with me, all right.

"You think I didn't do enough for him? For Terrence?"

Alonzo's almost out the door. I should let him leave. Let the matter drop. Honestly, we've never discussed how Terrence got killed and now isn't the moment.

The keys jingle in his hand. Then he grips them so hard his knuckles glow white under the glaring hotel lights. Bet they're cutting into his skin.

"He had issues," Alonzo says. "Issues that were bigger than you or me. If you're blaming yourself for something, you need to put that to rest."

"He was my twin brother. I should have known something was wrong. Where he was that day."

"Yeah, and he knew how to keep things from you when he wanted. He kept things from everyone. For real, man. Let it go."

There's no way that's ever going to happen. My brother was going through shit and I didn't know how to help. We were supposed to go through everything together. He's supposed to be here now, helping me get a passed-out white girl into this hotel.

The keys jingle again. Alonzo taps the hood of the car. "Keep an eye on Drunky Drunkerton back there. I'll go get us a room."

I reach for my wallet. "Let me."

He slaps me on the shoulder. "You bought food earlier."

A stupid waffle house meal costs way less than a room with two double beds. We both know the truth. That Alonzo drew the long straw and wound up with someone who left him an actual inheritance, and I've burned through most of the prize money I socked away. Still, I don't like sitting back and letting him pay.

He gives me a look. "Pick up breakfast in the morning. I'm gonna check us in before the weather gets ugly."

Then he shuts the door and I'm left sitting and waiting—something I can't stand—and wanting to put my fist through the window. I look into the back seat at Kate. At the moment, she looks damn near peaceful. The way her hair falls across her face. The way her chest rises and falls. I find myself watching for longer than necessary to make sure she's breathing okay.

I'm still looking when Alonzo returns with key cards and paperwork. "All right. We're on the third floor. I asked for a room by the elevator so we could get Princess Party Punch into bed."

"Great. Thanks. There a back entrance we can pull around to?"

Alonzo shrugs. "Locked after nine p.m. Short trip through the lobby, though."

Fool.

"Man, I don't know what you're thinking, but it's the middle of the night. You don't think two guys hauling an unconscious girl through the lobby might arouse some suspicions?"

"So fucking wake her up, man." Alonzo goes around to the driver's seat and pokes at Kate. When that doesn't work, he slaps at her face.

She mumbles something incoherent and smacks her lips. Then nothing.

I give him a look. "Next?"

"I think you're being paranoid. This isn't the fifties."

My gran would've smacked Alonzo and me both in the back of the head right about now. "And if I'm not? Anybody could see her like that and think we're the ones who got her into this state."

He's giving me the eye roll. "Okay. Fine. Night clerk's watching porn on his laptop. I'll flirt a little to distract him. We're cool."

"Your ideas are God-awful. What makes you think he's even into guys?"

"He's watching porn and it's the middle of the night. Even if he isn't, he'll be distracted enough to entertain the notion."

"This couldn't be a worse plan if it were thought up by Pinky and The Brain. Why in the hell can't you just let us in the back door?"

"*Hello.* It's locked. When you open a locked door after hours in a commercial building, there's usually an alarm. And I'm the one who doesn't think?"

I grumble and give up the argument. He could be wrong. And if he's not? That'd cause a hell of a lot more commotion. "If this goes sideways, I am kicking your ass."

"Really? Because I was thinking I'd be the one to bail you out if you got thrown in the pokey. You want me to carry her instead?"

Kate has never really and truly been mine. Kate, the girl she used to be, was a mine I didn't appreciate like

I should have. It would be a lie to call her a burden, although that's how I thought of her on occasion. That pesky little school girl who showed up at fights and wouldn't leave me alone.

Except wouldn't you know, that girl matured into a fine-looking young woman. Keeping my hands off her got harder as the months and years flew.

Then that beautiful young woman got into a car with my brother, and we don't know each other anymore. To this day, I don't know why she was with him. Or why she refused to see me after.

What I do know is, her not being mine anymore doesn't stop a deep snarl from forming in my chest when Alonzo reaches to pull her from the back seat.

"I'll get her out," I tell him in an angry growl. It's the gravel-low, threat-laden voice I bring out when I'm trying to psych out an opponent. Not when I want my foster brother to get his mitts off my girl.

My girl. Right.

Alonzo backs away from the car with his hands up the way someone would if they had a gun aimed their way. "Okaaay. I will hump our meager belongings up to the room and maybe hump the desk clerk a little on the way. You handle Mistress Droolsalot."

She's not drooling all that much. I swipe a tiny drop of moisture from her lip and pull her out of the back seat. Aside from some hmming and mumbling, there's no sign of life.

"Okay." I point to Alonzo. "Your plan better work."

I'm rewarded with an expression of fake innocence. "Did I say I have a plan?"

This is going to end well. I can feel it.

4. AWFULLY GROWN-UP

Ty

Alonzo's making friends with the vending machine down the hall. Lucky for all of us, his predication was correct and we made it past the night clerk without incident. Mostly without incident. Sort of.

Without incident unless you count the part where my stupid-ass best friend decided to freak out the clerk by offering him oral, and then running back to the scene of the crime while we're waiting for the elevator to raid that complimentary tray of chocolate chip cookies on the check-in desk.

"You're the biggest idiot I know," I'd said to him for maybe the millionth time since we'd known each other.

"Who says no to free cookies?" At which point he'd held one out like he expected me to take it while I was trying to keep a drunk Kate from sliding off my shoulder.

"They're probably stale anyhow."

"Hey. Free cookies are free cookies." Hard to understand him properly while he was chewing. Think that's what it sounded like he said.

Doesn't matter now while I'm trying to figure out what to do with the hundred pounds of drunk girl passed out on my shoulder.

The process of laying her on the bed is awkward. Not only does she look uncomfortable, the way she's landed with her neck bent and her arms out to the side, but she's above the covers and I don't see how she can sleep in those clunky boots.

Clodhoppers, my gran would've called 'em.

Pulling off the boots is a whole process. There's about a zillion laces to loosen. It's amazing she hasn't woken up yet, and here I am tugging and jiggling her feet to get these damn things off her.

I'm appalled at the sight of her socks, the kind that used to be fluffy and warm but now are worn thin with holes. For Aspiration, this girl's family does all right. Or so I thought. Have the medical bills been that bad?

When she shivers on top of the bed, I look around and rub my forehead with frustration. She needs warmer clothes. She needs *clean* clothes. The bottoms of her cargo pants are muddy from being out in that field. It would kill me to have to wake her, but…

She rolls onto her back. On the way over in the car, she took off the sweatshirt I loaned her. Now the flop of her arms and the splay of her legs don't leave a lot to the imagination. Okay. At the least, I have to get her under the covers. Ideally before Alonzo comes back. I don't think he thinks of her that way, but the guy's a horndog and I'd rather not even go there.

Besides, it's not like I never saw her body. Not never, but not much, and that was back…before. For a whole host of reasons, this feels like a huge difference.

All the same, I tell myself this is no different than if Alonzo was passed out drunk. I flip the privacy lock, grab a pair of my sweats and a shirt from my bag, and get to peeling away her dirty clothes. I'd get something from her bag, but I don't like rummaging around in someone else's stuff.

Even with the lights dim, it's easy to see all of her scars up close. The angry, raised-up skin, the pink and the reddish-tan places that still look inflamed after having so much time to heal.

Some things take more than time to heal, I guess.

It's almost like the flames from where the car caught fire are still licking their way up her flesh. Permanently burned there into her body.

Hell. Hard enough for *me* to let go. I lost my brother that day. My mirror. Half my heart and soul. She had to sit right beside him and watch him die, and she'll wear the evidence forever.

When she stirs and murmurs something in her sleep, I realize I've been touching her in a way I never should have. Running my fingers over the marks that climb her rib cage, marveling at how she's even alive. Wondering why she doesn't seem to care that she is.

As I'm about to pull away, her hand slides over mine. One quick squeeze, before flopping back to the bed. If I'd had anything to drink myself tonight, I might think I'd imagined the instant exchange.

It's impossible to quit staring. At the way her long, dark lashes lay over her cheeks. Her body, the one that always seemed plastered with unseen "Forbidden" signs, no longer looks like it belongs to a teenager. That body's looking awfully grown-up.

"Dude, what the hell?"

I jump at the bang of the door lock. "Dammit. Hang on."

I throw a Roy's Gym T-shirt on over her body before Alonzo has a chance to get pissy out in the hall. It was given to me by heavyweight boxing champ Dante Ramos when I visited the gym he co-owns in Evergreen

Grove, and it seems less weird than giving her one I wear all the time. Less familiar.

Alonzo slaps the room door. "Man, I gotta take a piss."

"So hold it like a big boy." There's no way to get the shirt smoothed over her shoulders, her arms, her back without touching. Without my fingers along her skin. Without my nose taking in a hint of her smell—her real smell, not the lingering stench of a rave—and *hell* no I am not boning up right now.

The door thumps again. "I'm gonna come in there and do my pee pee dance right in front of you."

Well. That sure took care of things.

I pull the cover over Kate and let Alonzo inside. "Stupid ass. I'm trying to keep her from waking up and you're out there trying to wake the entire floor."

Alonzo bustles past me, dropping half a machine's worth of candy bars on the bed. "Whatever. She's lucky I caught her before she took any of those muscle relaxers she was trying to score. She could be in a coma for days. God forbid I was right and that chick really was a narc."

I'd rather not consider the possibilities, but I'm finding it hard not to. So instead I chuck one of the candy bars at Alonzo. "Thought you had to piss."

"Yeah, yeah. I'm going." He pokes at her leg through the ugly-looking green and tan blanket. "Relax. Your girl's fine."

"She's not my girl. She was never my girl." True words. Sort of. Maybe.

"Yeah? So why'd you come along on this little road trip again?" Alonzo chucks the candy bar back at me. Huh. Mounds. I open it up and take a bite.

"Looking out for a friend. Same as you."

"A friend. Okay." Alonzo makes a noise in his throat and then closes the bathroom door in my face.

I look back at Kate sleeping on the bed and try to focus on getting myself changed. "We're friends," I say again.

No one's listening though. And I'm back where she and I first started, wondering if it's even my place to protect her.

#

Kate

I have no idea what time it is when I wake. Feels like morning but I'm in the dark, literally, in an unfamiliar place.

I'm alone…ish. The soft snores one bed over must be Alonzo's, because I almost step on Ty when I'm making my way to the bathroom.

Everything hurts. Of course it does. When I manage to slink home and sneak inside after a party, I've got things covered. Painkillers and antacids and a shower, and usually I even manage to wake up with my money back in my purse the next morning.

I have a fuzzy memory of flashing lights. My mother yelling. Jumping into a strange car. Which must be how I wound up here, with Alonzo and Tyler in what looks, as my eyes adjust, like a decently nice hotel room.

Memory is spotty sometimes since the accident. Drinking doesn't help. A smarter person would quit, but my mama didn't raise no quitter. A stubborn malcontent, sure. Not a quitter.

The sudden flash of bathroom light is way evil to my sensitive vision and pounding head. "Oh. Hey. Uncool."

I sink to the floor and ball myself up on a fuzzy bath mat, only slightly grateful for the pounding in my skull. I get killer hangovers, which is either coincidence or somehow related to my head injury. I've never asked because there's no way that *so, doc, seems like most kids my age party 24/7 with little consequence, but when I drink my weight in vodka it feels like someone's drilling a hole in my skull. Can we do anything about that?* is going to go over well with any legit physician.

At the least, it takes my mind off the way my back sometimes feels like it belongs to an eighty-year-old, too weak and too achy to hold me up. The way my leg stiffens when I walk and my neck seizes if I turn my head too far to the side. The way regular hook-behind-the-back bras feel like a modern-day torture device because my arm no longer bends the right way to put them on. No way it's healthy, but when I drink, my body is loose. I can move more like the way I used to, and I don't guard every turn and muscle twitch.

On the con side…

"The morning after's a real bitch, huh?"

Ty's voice floats over me, massaging my aches. Since the accident, things sound different. I notice a texture and a color to noises that didn't pass my awareness before. Some things, like my old band's music, don't resonate well with me anymore.

Ty's voice, though? Soft. Light. Sturdy.

Comforting. The color of sunrise.

I groan but I don't bother to look up at him. He kindly turns the light off and props his phone next to the sink so there's only a gentle glow by which to see.

"I'd feel embarrassed," I say. "But I don't recall starting the night in a T-shirt five sizes too big. So it would seem you've already witnessed me in some sort of compromising position."

Oh, whatever. Ty's seen me at my worst. This night doesn't hold a candle to my worst. Once you've been informed that you flatlined for twenty-seven seconds, there is no other bottom. You've crash landed, my friend.

Fuck, have you ever.

I've gotten really good at swearing lately. Started out as a thing because I wanted to piss off my mom, and ended up being a fun way to vent my frustrations.

Ty reaches over and turns on the water. "Now see, this right here is what I call a prime opportunity. All the free hot water you could ask for, premium water pressure, and no waiting for one of your other six housemates to get their asses out so you can get stuck with cold water."

Yikes. "I don't need a shower."

"You said you did before. And no offense, but my nose tells me otherwise. Come on. You'll feel more human after you rinse off the party grime." His fingers brush under my arms. I know firsthand exactly how large those hands are and what he can do with them. I've seen him punch through boards, blocks, and guys whose heads appeared to be made from said substances. Those same hands have the power to rest on my skin lighter than any feather, as they're doing now.

He's going to make me stand. I don't want to, but I don't want to fight with him. Not that he'd ever hurt me. Not with his hands, anyway. His words have always had the power to knock me down.

One arm cradles me. As tired and sore as I am, I'm dying to simply rest my head on his arm. The shower turns on. Its spray hits the inside of the tub with sharp, painful strikes that resonate in my head like white lightning.

"Ow," I mumble against the mound of his biceps.

"This is just a suggestion, but…maybe if you don't brine your gray matter until it's screaming for mercy, you wouldn't be hurting so much right now. Just saying." He's quiet. That glowing sunlight in his tone a whisper of warmth over my skin. A tickle on the back of my neck.

Maybe if you hadn't left me alone and broken when we needed each other most, I wouldn't be hurting so much right now. Just saying.

I push away from the safety of his arm and stand in front of him, holding his stare while I strip off the shirt someone put on me in my sleep. I figure it was him. Mostly because it's an advertisement for some gym and Alonzo never set foot in any gym in his life. Not unless he was there to see Terrence box.

Ty assumes his signature stance. Legs wide, arms crossed, smug smile. The way he'd face off with an opponent back when he did that street fighting stuff. They never shook hands or any of those other things that masqueraded as sportsmanlike conduct, the way I always thought they ought to do.

Funny thing, if he hadn't been trying to keep one of his opponents from following me home, we might never have ended up where we are now. I don't know if that's good or bad.

It *is,* I guess. That's all. It just *is.* "You're just going to stand there?" I'm challenging him. I know I am. He clearly knows it, too.

He's also clearly not taking the bait. *Or* leaving. There was a time he worried so much about being careful. If anyone did the pushing, it was me.

I guess I'm still the one pushing. Difference is, this time he's not turning away. Maybe he's changed, too, after all.

"I'm making sure you don't do anything stupid." He tips his head. "Anything *else* stupid."

"Making sure I don't do anything stupid could be a full-time job, Ty. Not sure you're up for those hours."

He shakes his head.

I pull off my sports top. My scars are surely visible this close up, even in the dim light he's created in the bathroom. Also, my breasts. He doesn't hide that he's looking, but he doesn't make a move.

Except to offer me his back.

I'm not surprised. I think I'm also kinda bummed. It would be nice to think someone believed I was still pretty enough to be worth watching or even touching when it's not dark and mind-altering substances aren't involved. Ty and I never did get to the really good stuff. He was always so afraid of hurting me. Of disrespecting me.

Damn those good guys and their morals.

"Hey." I push off my boy shorts, standing by the tub as steam fills the small space between us. "Hand me the little bottles of shampoo and conditioner, will you?"

Honestly, I might still be drunk. Or deluding myself. Possibly both. Probably both. Because this feels like a world-class performance. I started this little striptease to try to mess with his head. The guy who broke my heart and left me feeling three inches tall. Now he's eyeballing me over his shoulder and I'm caught in the tractor beam of his stare while he reaches with his long, muscular arm to the vanity counter and hands me two little bottles without missing a beat. Or looking away.

"I'll wait right here. Make sure you don't need anything."

"I can take a shower, Ty. I've been doing that on my own for a long time."

He looks at me like I'm a kid who got caught hiding something they stole. "Still. I'll be right here."

"Fine."

Just to make things painful, I reach up to hang my towel over the top bar before stepping under the spray. When he reaches to help, I bat his hand way. "Let me do my own stuff."

I shoot him a glare and get in, noting that he glances over his shoulder one more time before I pull the curtain.

5. FAKE STUFF

Ty

I stick to my stubborn-ass-guns for as long as I can stand. And Lord, can I be stubborn. My gran always said between me and an angry bull, she didn't know who'd win in a showdown.

I used to say I'd break that bull's skull.

When the bathroom clouds up with steam so thick I can't see my own hands, I'm ready to get on out of there. Especially after the water stops running. I don't need a repeat of that strip show from before.

Do I want one? Hell yes, I do.

But no. Nothing good would come of something like that happening now.

"Hey, can you hand me another—"

Before she can finish, I've balled up an extra towel and dunked it over the bar. "You're welcome."

"Hey! You hit me right in the head."

"Good. You can dry your hair. I'll be out in the hall. Restaurant next door opens early. When you're finished, we can find breakfast."

Me? I need some air. Now.

She meets me in the hall outside our room ten minutes later, back to wearing the T-shirt I put on her and a pair of what must be her own sweats. Me having a hundred pounds on her should mean she looks ridiculous. That shirt swallows her whole.

But she doesn't look ridiculous. All I can feel is a strange sort of grabbing and pulling in my gut. She's wearing my clothes, tied a knot in one side to make it tight around her hips. That tiny, curvy body of hers is all wrapped up in something I gave her. Once again that heart I thought I didn't have is racing right straight for things I shouldn't want.

"I guess Alonzo isn't coming?"

I nod to our locked room door. Our friend's rumbling snores are loud enough to come through, sounding like an industrial engine. "You wanna go back in and wake him?"

Not that Alonzo wouldn't provide some good distraction. Kate and I haven't exactly had any kind of significant alone-time since…well. Since the morning of Terrence's funeral, when I stopped by her hospital room to see her first.

Nothing good about that day.

She shakes her head though, and in spite of my thoughts I'm strangely relieved. There's no question we've got a world of issues between us. Maybe it's best if we step into those things head-on. Shine a light, as my gran would say, because ugliness lives in the dark.

"Ty?"

I'm staring. Hard not to. There may have been a time when the closest thing we had to a date was me walking her home to make sure she got there safe, but even during the dark times I never stopped caring.

"Ty?"

Still staring. *Get it together, brother.* Sometimes I swear I can still hear Terrence's voice.

I shake my head and pass her to go down the hall. "Need coffee. Zoned out."

"O…kay…"

I clap my hands together. "Yeah. Coffee. Bacon. Waffles. Here we go. You coming?"

Even though she shrugs and follows, she doesn't look convinced. She's still looking at me like I grew wings and a tail when we get our food at the restaurant twenty minutes later. "So I thought you were getting waffles?"

She's pointing to my omelet.

Come on. Six eggs. Green pepper. Steak *and* bacon. Sausage on the side. "Look at this thing. You can't pass up a helping of protein like this. And…"

The waitress puts down her meal. Two waffles. Side of bacon. Two eggs over hard. Buttered toast. A lot has changed but no way has Kate developed a sudden ability to eat like a lumberjack. I grab one waffle with my fork and drag it to my plate. "Bam!"

"Hey." She's frowning, but I can't say she looks that mad. Which is good for me.

"No way you were gonna eat all that," I say around a bite of waffle. Oh, man. It's got artificially flavored syrup, too. I know real maple's the thing, but Gran put the fake stuff on our breakfast when we were kids. I love that stuff. Don't tell me how bad it is.

She crosses her arms over her chest and gives me the look of death. It lasts all of thirty seconds before she gives in and starts on her bacon. "Okay, sure. Have my waffle. But a little warning would be nice."

"You saw the fork coming."

"Yeah, well, maybe next time you'll see my foot coming."

"I look forward to that meeting." With a wink and smile, I'm back to focusing on my food. Alonzo may be able to eat out of vending machines, but I don't roll that way. Foster care introduced me to the trials of hit-or-miss food. Got spoiled by my gran's cooking though, when I was a kid.

So I'm busy digging into my eggs with meat and more meat when her boot collides with my shin. Too hard to be an accident.

"Oof." I cough hard, but I'm too busy chewing a large mouthful to retaliate.

"So. There you are. The meeting you so anticipated. Was it good for you?" She's leaning forward. One hand propping up her chin. That sweet smile on her face shows me a ghost of Kate—that cute girl I used to walk home after school.

I have to swallow my bite. Quickly, against the bubbling urge to laugh. "Yeah, all right. Point goes to you."

This feisty new Kate, she's got an edge. She's angry. Quite possibly, she has a drinking problem. There's a spark in there though, a fire in those eyes I don't remember from before.

Imagine my surprise when I realize I might like this new version of the girl I used to love.

#

Kate

I've only heard of Evergreen Grove thanks to Alonzo. We follow each other on Instagram. His pictures don't do the little town justice though, considering they're mostly selfies taken inside his house (*Beer pong time, people!*) or some bar called Joe's (*Time for beer and darts, people!*) or this one diner right outside of town that's apparently open late just for guys like him (*Drunk munchies and milkshakes, people!*).

"It's cute," I mumble mostly to myself.

It is, though. In spite of their similar size, it's nothing at all like Aspiration.

We're driving down Main Street around midday. Seriously. There's an actual Main Street. With bricks on the road. And tiny little shops. Like Mayberry or something, but without the inept sheriff's deputy. At least not that I know of.

The town's got a suspiciously sweet, comfortable feel. It gives me the shivers.

In all the years I lived there, Aspiration never felt like home. What are the chances that this place really could?

Alonzo's nodding from the front seat. He's wearing shades, which I only hope are for the sun's glare and not because he smoked up while Ty and I were going to the bathroom at the last rest stop. "We'll do a little tour later. There's some cool stuff in town. I figured first we'd drop you at my place. Let you meet Layla. See about where you can crash. Layla and Angie were sharing, so you could probably bunk with her."

About that. "Hey, no offense, but Ty mentioned your place is sort of crowded."

Alonzo snorts. "Ain't so bad. Right, Ty?"

Next to Alonzo, Ty shrugs, mute and stoic once again in the passenger seat.

I point an accusing finger at Ty. Like we're in a crime drama and it's my job to shout out the whodunit. "You said you're sleeping on the basement floor."

"Not the floor. There's an army cot."

"Oh, well that's much better. Sign me up for that. *No* and by the way *absolutely not,* guys. Not to sound like a precious princess, but I've got back pain on top of back pain since the accident. And migraines. When I get one, I need to be able to sleep somewhere quiet. Is there maybe a hotel around here or something? If it seems like I'm going to stick around, then maybe I can look into something more permanent."

The silence is literally painful. Or maybe the pain is because Alonzo hit a pothole.

They look back and forth at each other. I can see they're both thinking about what I said. That it hadn't entirely sunk in for them that after all this time, I'm not back to normal. It hasn't occurred to anyone. Even my physical therapist was starting to wonder why I hadn't healed more yet, but the fact is I'm still in pain.

Everything hurts. Every day.

I do my best to ignore it. Some days I almost can. Although…I'll admit there's a little panic when I can't get my hands on anything to numb out.

"Uh." Alonzo half coughs, half clears his throat. "So there used to be a motel but it's more of a halfway house or something now, I think? Not sure that's a workable solution, but my roommate knows the guy who runs it, so we could check it out."

Sounds like a plan to inconvenience a lot of people. "What else?"

"There's a bed and breakfast up on The Ridge. Only a few rooms, but given that it's not tourist season, you might have luck there. Pretty fucking ka-ching, if you ask me. I think there might also be a hotel the next town over, closer to the college."

Ah, but I bet that B&B has great beds. Maybe even a big bathtub I could soak in. My mom's house only has a stand-up shower so I literally haven't taken a bath in ages. I think I'd offer indecent favors to strangers for a bath.

"Sold. Take me to the B&B, baby."

Ty turns around and looks at me like I'm crazy. "You don't want to hear any other options?"

"*Are* there other options? A hotel in a college town sounds busy and loud."

They glance at each other again. "Any buddies you know?" Ty scratches his elbow. His one tiny sign of uncertainty.

"I think my roommate's friend and her boyfriend have a house in town. They probably have a spare room or know someone who does."

I roll my eyes. "Boys, I have a head injury. Sometimes I don't have a filter and yet I still have more tact than to consider that plan. Nobody wants a random stranger crashing at their house. Take me to…to…the other place."

Damn. My memory is having a cloudy day. It's like, the word is right there but it's suddenly obscured from view. Usually if I wait a few seconds it comes back. Sometimes it doesn't.

"The B&B?"

"Yes! That one. Make it so."

"Careful, Kate." Alonzo looks over his shoulder when we reach a Stop sign. "Your nerd is hanging out."

I blow him a raspberry. "*You* caught the reference."

Ty sighs, heavy and put upon. "You're both children."

Perhaps, but at least our silly bantering distracts me from the way my back muscles are ratcheting tighter and tighter. If it takes us much longer to get where we're going, I may simply throw the car door open and jump out. Faster and more effective, right? Can't possibly be any more painful.

Alonzo looks into the rearview. "So definitely the B&B then?"

"I can afford a night or two in a place with lacy duvet covers," I tell them.

I haven't really spent any of my settlement money. One of the reasons I stayed living at home was to hang onto my bank balance until I knew for sure what I wanted to do. Much to my mom's chagrin. Not the living at home part, but the money part. I think my dad's concern that Mom would give all of it away was valid.

What I'd be doing now in that case, I'm not sure.

I've only dipped into the fund once before, and that was to buy clothes and supplies for a homeless dude who used to hang out near my favorite used bookstore before it closed. We don't get a lot of super cold nights in South Carolina, but on a rare one when the temp dipped below freezing, I couldn't handle seeing Redmond Otis curled on the sidewalk bench wearing nothing but a light army jacket and worn sneakers.

Other nights I'd let my mom foot the bill for bringing him hot soup and coffee, buying the food at the grocery store from cash she kept in a little tea tin in the kitchen. So the guilt money from that accident is money I know I'll need to use more, I just hate it. I hate needing it, and I hate *why.*

As we're heading out of downtown, Ty pipes up. "You guys can let me out here. I need to take care of a few things. Alonzo, you head on over to get our girl checked in."

Our girl?

I'd choose to take that as some sort of possessive statement, but knowing Ty, it's simply a statement of friendship. Maybe? I don't know. Getting your head whacked into glass at fifty miles an hour tends to mess up your logical reasoning skills.

Alonzo raises his eyebrows. "We can swing by and grab something after—"

"Nah. Just let me out here."

Alonzo pulls over, still giving him a look. "If you're sure."

Ty gives us both a wave. "See you after a while. Have fun with all the doilies."

I almost laugh. Almost. After we pull away again, I ask, "What's with him?"

Alonzo shrugs. "The B&B is in this big old Victorian house up on The Ridge, right between a mansion that converted into an art gallery and a huge house that belongs to some elderly lady. The mayor's house is on the same road. It's the rich people part of town, you know? Those of us who came up in the system kinda get hives when we come too close to those folks."

It's not as if I grew up in some obscene golden tower. But I get what he means all the same. "But you're going?"

"Yeah. You're lucky I love you."

"Right. Why are you really going?"

Alonzo shrugs. "Keep asking and maybe I'll draw a map on a fast food napkin and make your ass walk."

I hold up my phone. "I do have GPS, old buddy." Seriously, though. I don't want to walk and I hope he knows I'm screwing with him.

He sticks his tongue out at me again and makes a left at the next stop sign. "Don't tempt me. *Buddy*. Seriously though. You're going to flip when you see this place. It's out of control."

I mumble something in agreement. For as long as I can, I watch Ty jog down the opposite block away from us.

6. IT ISN'T LADYLIKE

Ty - Then

Back in my early fighting days—even when my technique needed work—my size and my speed and my left hook gave me a good advantage. Fewer weaknesses in a match meant more guys coming from farther away to sniff out a challenge. Hell, I liked it like that. More guys looking for a fight meant more money in my pocket.

Until Kate started coming around. Kate, it turned out, was my major weakness. Had I been smart, I'd have slammed my foot down about her not coming to watch me fight. But like my gran said, even a smart man can let his wants make him stupid. Besides, I was never sure how in the hell I was supposed to make her stay away.

Still, it bit me hard the day a big dude named Eliot Ness came over from Elloree to have the honor of putting my face in the dirt. Standing six-seven and two-oh-two—which was at the time a little more than I weighed—Ness had the size advantage. That fight drew a crowd. Shop owners and passersby who usually turned a blind eye to what we did in that lot poked their heads out to see what would happen. But I held my own like I always did.

Taller than me? Fine. Leg locks. Kidney punches. Rolls. Takedown.

"The bigger they come the harder they fall, son!" I'd shouted when the man tried to take me in a headlock and instead got laid out on his back.

Didn't even care if it had been the most tired-ass taunt in the history of taunts. Followed up that throw with a body slam and an elbow to the kidneys. Adrenaline flew through my body. That fight was in the bag. My brother was out there collecting bets for me, so I'd eat well that night. Everything was good. Everything was *damn* good.

Until I looked up from that body slam and saw Kate. Out there on the edge of the crowd, she'd been watching for I didn't know how long. What I did know was the thug moving up on her had recently done a three-year bid for assaulting his girlfriend. Milton Goins had gone on a drunken rampage and been on that poor girl like she was his opponent in the octagon, breaking her leg and rearranging her pretty face.

No way in hell was that sick psycho allowed to touch Kate.

My distraction cost me. Ness took his opening and flipped our positions. Threw me onto my back with a head-ringing thud.

"Oh, who's down now, motherfucker?" He practically sang it to me.

Problem. I had a huge fighter on top of me, rearing back and ready to knock me out. From the corner of my eye, I had a girl I cared for, getting touched by a man who'd proven himself dangerous. Getting KO'd was not an option.

When Ness came in for the kill, I caught his arm and pushed it across his body. Trapped his neck between my thighs. Then I pulled his head down with my left hand and I twisted my hip to the right, cutting off the air and blood supply to his neck until he tapped out. Triangle choke. Wasn't pretty, but it worked.

The second it was over I was on my feet. Without a word, I pulled Kate away from the crowd, ignoring Goins's protests. When he persisted, I turned on him with a quiet directive.

"That will be the last time you touch her, look at her, or even come near her. I won't tell you twice."

And Goins, smug from his time inside no doubt, had only laughed. "What can you do to stop me?"

"You don't want to find out." Neither did I. Didn't want to break any promises to my gran about avoiding jail time.

After that, I'd walked Kate directly home without our usual lazy strolling or conversation.

"Ty, what are you mad about? I didn't do anything. I didn't even talk to him, okay? He talked to me. I stood there and watched you fight like usual, that's *all*."

The entire fifteen-minute walk to her house she kept up a steady stream, professing her innocence and denying any wrongdoing. While my heart wanted to forgive, somewhere deep inside, some potent mix of fear and rage held me back. I'd been out on the street the day they took Trinity, Goins's girlfriend, to the hospital. Her face looked like raw hamburger. Kate had no clue what she'd been near.

Finally, at the end of Kate's street, I turned. "Remember when I told you not to come around those fights anymore?"

A stain of red flashed across her cheeks. "Yeah, but I thought you meant…you know, like my mother tells me not to drink from the bottle because it isn't ladylike. I don't care about being ladylike."

"Goins just got out of prison for assault and battery. And I nearly lost that fight because I couldn't focus while I was worried about what might happen to you around him. Do you understand? It's dangerous for you and it's dangerous for me."

Kate's not the palest girl I've ever seen, but when the blood all drained from her face? Looked like the ghost of Kate past. When her ankles wobbled and her lip trembled, I wanted to take back everything I'd said.

I wanted to, but I couldn't have the likes of Milton Goins sniffing around her anymore.

"Oh." The one syllable came out in such a soft whisper I hardly heard. "Sorry."

She didn't cry, but a breathy hiccup echoed from her chest. I sat us down behind a big oak tree on the corner and pulled her to me. We sat while I held her head against my chest. While I soaked up her warmth and assured us both everything would work out okay if she just didn't come by the fights anymore.

I even believed the lie. But it changed everything between us. In some ways, it was a beginning. In others, it was the beginning of the end.

#

Ty

One thing I've always been able to do is run. I can put my head down through anything, and power through the pain. Served me well after Gran died. After Terrence and I got split apart, and again after he died. It's not serving me so well now, when every step reminds me that nothing in Evergreen Grove takes longer than twenty minutes to jog to, and I could easily change my route to go and check on Kate.

Seeing her again. Hell. I needed a little distance just to be able to think.

It's Tuesday, two mornings after Alonzo and I returned from our ridiculous mission to get her out of trouble, and I'm out for a long one in hopes that the cold will clear my head. Not freezing, but cold enough that my man parts sure wish they had a better place to hide than sweats and a down vest over my T-shirt.

The vest I borrowed from Alonzo. My twenty pounds more of muscle and his preference for tight clothes aren't doing me favors this fine morning. Each time I think of buying myself some gear, I think nah, I'll leave town soon. To where, I never decided.

Can't stay here forever. Much as I love Alonzo, there's not a ton for me in Evergreen Grove, a town that appears even smaller than Aspiration. In spite of the prettier packaging.

I've picked up a few fights nearby for cash. Living with my friend keeps things cheap. Still, no man wants to freeload forever.

I pass the town line and cross over into Pender where there's a small college campus. The quaint limestone buildings and sprawling green pathways (Even in the winter! What do they do to the grass here?) speak to a place that probably charges more in tuition for a credit hour than I've earned in a single year.

Nice homes dot the perimeter of campus. I'm betting professors and whatnot mostly live here. A few apartments, but not like where I come from. No cramped buildings with creaky stairs and unemployed old men camping out on the steps. Or unemployed young men drinking their breakfast. Here it's cute little converted houses with only four units, if I'm counting doors right, and they each look to be about the size of the house I grew up in. Each clearly holds multiple students.

For about a minute I wonder how much they cost. "No damn way," I mumble. That sort of wondering only gets me in trouble.

Last time I dared to dream of a future, I lost everything.

In spite of there being a really good hill to work my legs and lungs, I decide to avoid The Ridge when I cross back into Evergreen Grove. After taking a couple of days to recover from the car trip, Kate is supposed to be doing a look-see around town with Alonzo today. It's better if I save myself the heartburn of seeing her when I'm unprepared. Again.

Yesterday I was determined to do nothing but eat chips and watch hockey on the couch.

She was standing between me and my favorite onion dip when I went to the store. I left before she saw me, but the dizziness remained. Now how's a man supposed to properly enjoy his cheat-day without ridged potato chips and onion dip? He can't, not if running into the girl who makes his head spin still has it spinning hours later.

Even though I don't climb the hill to where the pretty people sip champagne and eat caviar, the houses loom in my line of sight over the edges of the trees. I still see them from down on Main Street. The fancy spiral lighting thing on top of the gallery looks cool. That's what I focus on. Not the house next door and the fact that a girl I once took for granted would be waiting for me is up there…maybe still waiting on me but probably not.

I try to tell myself it's ego. That I'm not in love with the girl anymore. Can't stand her being here in this town, but moving on without me.

Like my gran used to say, that bull stinks so bad the neighbor's gonna complain.

I've loved Kate since the first time I saw her, standing outside the circle of spectators while I was fighting. To this day I'm amazed she didn't run off.

"Nice girl like you shouldn't be around here," I'd told her.

"Then they shouldn't put the library so close by," she'd replied with a sunshiny grin.

Haven't gotten such a bright smile out of her since that accident.

The smell of smoke from a fireplace hits me as I jog through downtown Evergreen Grove. People are starting their day, cooking breakfast. Doing all those homey things that people in Norman Rockwell paintings do, I guess. I put my head down and focus on the strike of my feet on the pavement.

Those smells stir up hunger in my belly. The hunger drives me forward. It's a welcome reminder of my gratitude. Was a time I had no choice but to go out and use my fists if I wanted to eat. Crashing in Alonzo's basement these days is a damn luxury. Man's useless at buying groceries, but the upside is his beer-drinking roommates won't touch my kale and chicken breasts.

As I jog past a nursing home and then a mostly empty park, the few people I pass actually wave. No joke. The mailman, Walt, calls out a "good morning."

Evergreen Grove sure is friendlier than Aspiration.

The Ridge where Kate's staying is out of my sight now, blocked by trees and the storefronts of downtown Evergreen Grove. That doesn't stop me from looking in that direction and wondering if she's okay. Wondering how long she's actually gonna stay around here. Wondering how long I will.

I'm still wondering when Dante Ramos steps out of a storefront. Damn. Didn't even realize I'd been approaching Roy's Gym. I glance around, but there's no chance he didn't see me.

"Looking for a place to hide?"

Yeah. I fully grasp the irony that one of the things I've wanted like air this past year is to resolve what happened to Terrence before he died. After I found Dante, a man who worked with the same corrupt boxing trainer-turned-promoter Terrence worked with, I'm now uncomfortable speaking to him.

"Nah, I…" *Realized I'm not actually ready to talk about my brother. And that knowing what happened to him also happened to you makes me uncomfortable in your presence, even if it shouldn't.* "I'm distracted. This girl I used to know is in town. It's complicated."

Something I learned from my brother, even if I learned what he was doing too late. You hardly ever need to lie. All you need to do is tell a different truth.

Dante chuckles and crosses his thick arms over his chest. He may not get in the ring professionally anymore, but he's still got the guns to take a guy down.

"So you've kept up with your martial arts training?"

The question takes me off guard. I'd been expecting him to pelt me with questions about my brother's history with that monster, Arlo. After a second to clear my head, I roll my shoulders and force a more casual smile.

"Oh, you know. I practice as much as I can." Some of Alonzo's roommates are students so they get me into the gym over at the college campus for free when they can, and sometimes I just do forms out in Alonzo's yard. Training around other folks' schedules is tricky.

From the casual nod of his head, I can't tell what he thinks of my answer. Maybe I shouldn't care since I don't even know why he asked, but this is Dante Ramos. He's a big deal, and not just in this tiny town. I do care.

"Sounds good enough. You can always train here."

"Good enough?" And train there for what?

"Sure. How are you with kids?"

"Uh…I used to be one?" What the hell do I know about kids? Except for back in foster homes, I haven't been around anyone small.

"Great. You're hired."

There's no doubt my eyes are bugging. "Excuse me?"

As we're standing there, a massive pickup pulls up to the curb and a skinny white dude jumps out wearing a shiny pink winter coat. The really puffed-up kind. "Dante! Check out the new truck."

"Nice. Looks like a handful."

The man bobs his head. "It sucks gas like crazy, but it's hella fun to drive. It was a Valentine's Day gift from Hayden so I can't be too mad about the price tag. I've been needing a big vehicle to haul things around for odd jobs."

"Tell your man he's making the rest of us look bad. Next year I'm gonna feel obligated to buy Michelle a fleet of yachts or something." Dante nods to me. "AJ, this is Tyler. He'll be teaching that new kids' martial arts class we were talking about."

"Oh. Hey. Sweet!" Skinny Dude comes over and pumps my hand so enthusiastically, you'd think Dante introduced me as the guy who cured stupid. "It is so great to meet you. My daughter, Abby, she's been dying to take a class. She loves Jackie Chan movies. Wants to beat up all the bad guys. She's only in kindergarten; do you think that's too young?"

I turn to look at Dante, wishing I could communicate with my eyes the way I used to with Terrence. Willing my glare to ask him, *Dude, what the hell? Why am I here? Since when did I agree to teach some kids' class?*

I'm not even sure I like kids.

But maybe Dante gets it because he looks back with something that hand to God reads like, *Hey, remember that thing we were just talking about? Congratulations. You're going to teach a kids' martial arts class.*

This AJ guy is chattering about something, but I've lost it. "Anyway, what do you think?"

He's looking at me again. Right, because I'm the supposed teacher for some class that I didn't know existed. "Uh, yeah. Should be…okay." Maybe that covers all my bases.

He slaps me on the arm. "Great. Thanks. She'll be so excited to meet you."

"Can't wait."

"Awesome." We shake hands.

That awkward dead air thing happens, so I look for something to fill the void. "Yeah, nice truck by the way."

"I do kind of love it. Just need to add some glitter and ribbon to really butch it up."

I don't even know what to say here.

After a few seconds, AJ busts out laughing. "Man. Look at the way your mouth is hanging open. So easy to tell when folks are new around here."

I start to argue that I'm not that new. Then I realize correcting him will prolong a conversation that is only serving to turn my head inside out.

Dante waves AJ off. "Dude. Go home to your boyfriend. We'll see you later."

"Fine. You're no fun." He waves back and jumps in, pulling away with a low growl of engine and exhaust.

Many questions swirl in my brain. The foremost being, "I'm teaching a kids' class?"

Dante springs to life. "Come on, man. I could beg a lot, and tell you all about how I'm no good with kids, and I need you, or you could just take the job. It'll make both our lives easier."

On the one hand, I'm bristling and being railroaded into something I don't especially want to do. On the other, I've been sponging off Alonzo and slowly using my savings. It'd be nice to have a regular paycheck.

Except the thing is, I don't want to. Little kids looking up to me? I'm not so sure that's anything good.

Dante must see my hesitation. "Give it a try. Please. I know I put you in a tight spot but you can quit anytime. Worst case, I'll teach the rugrats if I have to."

"Careful. I'll rat you out to your fiancée for calling kids rugrats."

"Sure. Go right ahead."

"You sure she won't care that you were too scared to be in a room with some little kids?"

That sobers him up, and I know I said something wrong. I'm just not sure what. It was supposed to be a joke. Not that I know him well, but Dante Ramos doesn't seem bothered by much of anything. The fact that he is now drops a rock in my stomach.

If I rustle up the nerve to go public with what happened to Terrence, this is a guy I'll need on my side. Pissing him off is the last thing I want.

"Okay, listen. Sorry. I've never taught a class to kids before. Can I give it some thought?"

The mask of Dante's face breaks into a smile. "Sure, but don't think too long. Nothing worse than disappointing a bunch of elementary school students. That daughter of AJ's, she's damned adorable. And sassy. She'll give you a run for your money."

"Daughter. Right, he said that. But he has a boyfriend?"

"Yeah, that story's a bit complicated. Or not, really. Sometimes a boy and a girl like each other very much. Sometimes the boy likes other boys more." Dante shrugs. "They teach that lesson in health class, don't they?"

"Hell if I know. My brother and I were usually ditching class to earn, you know. Or play pranks. Especially in high school." It was the only time we got to see each other.

It was also the only way I could cheer Terrence up when he started to withdraw. I don't mention that now.

"I hear you." Dante fishes in his pocket for a business card. "Let me know something by next week. I'll teach the kids if I have to. It's my gym." He pegs me with a stare. "Don't make me have to. And get the hell back in here to train. I looked you up, you know. You haven't had a single pro fight since you went down for Marques. You weren't hurt bad enough to retire."

"Yeah, maybe I wanted to," I mutter.

I thought I did. At first I had big plans of rising up and showing the world what I could do. After Terrence died, my sense of direction faltered. Especially without Kate there to cheer me on.

"Not that it's any of my business, but I wonder what your brother would think about that."

Before I have a chance to let my anger at his intrusive comment boil over, a woman up the block yells "Morning, Dante!" We both turn to see a redheaded lady in a battered fur coat opening up the Laundromat next door to the gym.

"Oops, gotta go." Dante slaps me on the back. "That lady puts the 'Grr' in cougar. Tried telling her I'm engaged, but I'm not sure she cares. Watch your ass, buddy. I mean it literally. She's a pincher."

He demonstrates with a crab-claw hand gesture. Yeesh.

"Okay, but—" I give up on trying to ask more questions about this class he's roped me into, because Dante's disappearing inside the gym and that lady in the coat is headed my way. With a shake of my head, I resume my jog, not really sure what the hell just happened.

I'm wondering what Kate's doing and why she's the first person I want to talk to about this news I seem to have. What would she think of me teaching little kids?

Coat Lady's still coming. "Yoohoo! Tyler, right? I've seen you jog past my window! Hey!"

Damn. One thing I love about small towns. They put the crazy right out in the open, don't they? Still, I'm not sure I can handle much more of that right now.

7. WE'RE ALL SCREW-UPS.

Kate

Alonzo is late.

Way late. A little late, or even moderately late, would not be news. Alonzo is unclear about his heritage, but he jokes that his biological parents must have been from one of those places where they observed "island time." Appointments are more of a suggestion for him than a targeted time at which to arrive.

Still, he knows it bugs me and he promised he'd be here. Even for him, a couple of hours behind schedule is pushing the bounds of decency. I've straightened the room, called my father, and even flipped through some wine magazines to kill time. I'm about to throw in the towel on the awesome diner pancakes he promised me and go back to bed. Or worse, downstairs to the B&B dining room with that other couple and their chubby dachshund.

Aside from going to meet once with his friend and her band, I haven't left my room at the B&B. Honestly, after being stuck on my back in Mom's mausoleum for so long, I appreciate the rose and lace sanctuary at The Oak Tree Inn. It's quiet here, but peaceful quiet.

Still, I think Alonzo actually had a valid idea. There seems little point in coming to Evergreen Grove if I don't plan to get to know the town. So where the heck is he?

I've slept on a nice, firm king-sized mattress these past couple of nights. Aside from the fact that everything is done in some sort of Victorian style, this place isn't bad. There's a television hidden in a carved cabinet, a claw-foot bathtub and scented bubbles, which I've actually used a ton, and a wall of built-in bookshelves full of everything from some cute and appropriately small-town-ish romance novels by someone named Kristan Higgins to books on bread baking and winemaking, and even a hand-written book on the history of Evergreen Grove itself. The latter boggles my mind because apparently this town is so small that on the quaint little county map in my room, someone had to draw it in with a pen.

"Whatever, Alonzo. I give up, wherever you are." For all I know he's gone from hardly punctual to not even giving a shit. He could be passed out in his own drool somewhere.

I've got something called baked oatmeal waiting downstairs, according to a lovely young innkeeper named Sierra, and plenty more novels to flip through. Last night I finished the Lance Bass biography, which I can only assume a previous visitor left behind. Or maybe Sierra's into highly choreographed pop groups.

Hey, we love what we love and I'm not here to judge. Besides, I happen to enjoy a good five-part harmony. When everything blends perfectly, the music's like a rainbow.

I'm pulling on a super glamorous slouchy sweatshirt and leggings when my cell phone rings. I don't recognize the number, but maybe Alonzo's calling from his landline.

"Hey, girl. I owe you an apology."

Aha. "It *is* you. What's going on? You promised me breakfast at some awesome diner and I'm about to be forced to eat fancy brunch food over here."

"Sorry to hear about the indignities you've suffered, babe, but I kinda got arrested last night. No big, but I didn't want you to think I'd blown you off."

"Shit." What a bitch I am. I jerk at my own reflection as I pace alongside a standing mirror. "Where are you? Why didn't you call me earlier? I would have come to bail you out."

"Nothing for you to do, honey. Lieutenant Haas over here wanted me to sober up before I went anywhere. I'm fine. They'll let me out later and I can take you around town some other time."

"I'm going to come and get you, you moron. After that we're going to have a talk about the stupidity of getting wasted the night before you've got breakfast plans with your friend from out of town."

I think I hear him sigh over the phone. "Yeah. Noted. You really don't gotta come, though."

"Shut up, idiot. You guys came all the way to South Carolina to keep me from getting in trouble, didn't you? Didn't you? Or was that really mostly about keeping your roommate from kicking your ass."

I can tell he's still there, but he doesn't answer. The more I think about it, the more I want to believe it was the first thing.

"Alonzo."

"Yeah."

"I'll be there soon."

"Thanks, girl."

I roll my eyes and hang up the phone, but the second I do my head pounds. If I didn't feel so awful for Alonzo, I'd be pissed. The trouble is, losing Terrence killed us all. He was Ty's brother, I was in the car with him, but Alonzo? Alonzo's tried to keep us all in touch since it happened, and all we give him credit for is being a screw-up.

We're all screw-ups.

Either way, Alonzo's tried to be there for us in his misguided way, and I'm going to go help him. As soon as I figure out how. With a groan, I pull on my coat and head for the inn's big foyer. On the way, I dial the one person I know in this town who is not presently in the drunk tank.

"Yeah?"

"Hey, Ty. It's Kate."

"I know." The golden sunrise of his voice gives me an unexpected shiver.

"Yeah. Uh. So anyway, Alonzo and I were supposed to get together this morning but it turns out he's in some trouble. I could use your help."

#

Ty

"Don't see why we're rushing right over first thing. If all he's in for is drunk in public, they'll let him go eventually."

Kate's giving me a look like she wants to take my balls and make 'em into some fancy craft project. "So we should let him sit in an uncomfortable cell until then. Sure."

"I'm saying he got himself into this mess is all. Alonzo's got himself some issues lately. I'd love to help him but he won't share with the class."

Alonzo is my closest friend since I lost Terrence. It's not like I want him to suffer. Can't help but wonder though, if maybe having a consequence or two wouldn't encourage him to straighten up and fly right, as my gran would have said.

Kate shoots me another look. Sort of becoming her default. "And if it was one of us in there? What would he do?"

I close my mouth. She's right. I know exactly what Alonzo would do. Dude's made a hobby out of screwing up, but he does his best to be there for his friends. The first time he got transferred out of the foster home where we all met, he'd promised Terrence he'd be back for a teen boxing competition our social worker had set up. Alonzo snuck out and hitched a ride to get there. Also got kicked out of that placement in record time.

"Honestly," Kate continues, "if anyone but Alonzo had asked me to come to this half-horse town, I would've said no. I'm here, though, and my friend needs help, so we're helping."

I stop with my hand on the heavy outer door of the building. A carved wooden barrier that's about ten feet tall. With me leaning on it all she can do is yank on the handle and give me another angry look.

"What's your problem?" She lets go of the handle so she can put the question to me with her hands on her hips.

I'd laugh if this weren't serious. "That a real question?"

"No. That was a joke. The punchline involves a dirty limerick and a guy whose name rhymes with penis."

For a second I give her my back, not wanting her to see the involuntary smile tugging at my mouth. That was funny, but not funny enough to disarm my irritation. "My problem is you saying you'd only have come down here for Alonzo. I guess everything between you and me was nothing?"

Her eyes narrow. Damned if I can help the way that phantom thing in my chest kicks up its pace. She's angry—hell, she's probably plotting my untimely demise—and she's more beautiful than I've ever seen her. A gust of cold wind blows by, grabbing the hair that brushes her chin and pulling it back from her face. The pout of her lips and the dark swirl of her eyes have me feeling things I shouldn't. Things I walked away from and have no right to now.

"Maybe if you had contacted me even once since I've gotten out of the hospital, I'd think we still had the kind of relationship that meant we'd drop everything and help one another."

"Wha—We do. I *did.* How the hell do things escalate so fast with you?"

Kate crosses her arms and rolls her eyes. "I didn't need you at that party. I did need you when I was alone and scared in the hospital."

She has no idea how hard it was for me to stay away. "I did what I thought you wanted back then. What I thought would help you get better."

Somehow that's made her even angrier. "Let's just go get Alonzo."

She yanks on the door. This time I don't stop her from going in.

At one time, this girl had the power to pull me forward with nothing more than her smile. Then, the world exploded. The future I thought was in front of me… Well, I never did get back on track. Maybe I never stopped loving her, but I'm not sure how to handle having her this close to me right now. It burns, getting so close to this alternate version of the future I lost.

One more piece of the past I want badly to put right. But maybe I never can.

8. LEWD ACTS IN PUBLIC

Kate

Alonzo's not even in a cell when we get inside the station. He's perched on the desk of some busty brunette in a uniform, who is giving him her best "come hither" look.

"See, I think *Gone in Sixty Seconds* was really the height of Nicholas Cage's sex appeal, don't you?"

"I don't know," Alonzo says. "That one where he's some kind of corrupt police detective. You know, the boxing movie? I found him strangely appealing in that one."

Alonzo's looking up at the ceiling like he's giving the conversation real thought. She's twirling a small strand of hair by her ear that's escaped the bun at the back of her head. The whole thing is insane.

"Oh, good grief. I skipped breakfast for this?" Seriously. I'm not pretty when I'm starving, and by now I could eat my own arm. Or maybe Alonzo's.

I guess this is what I get for trying to help.

Behind me, a strangled noise says that Ty's trying not to laugh. Super. "Oh, buddy. Look out. The woman's hangry."

I turn and give him a nasty glare. "Yeah, I'll show you hangry in a minute."

Alonzo gives us a tired-looking wave. "Hey, girl. Told you there was no need to come all the way down here."

"I'll never doubt you again." That lie tastes like a bumpy, bitter lime rind on my tongue. I love Alonzo but he and I have both been a wreck since, well, the wreck. The faithful friend I once knew is a little shaky, but I'm in no place to judge.

A striking guy in uniform walks in, preoccupied with a stack of papers in one hand and a cup of coffee in the other. The kind of guy you expect to see playing a cop in movies, with exceptionally well-developed forearms and laser-sharp blue eyes. No doughnut belly or comedic bumbling for this small-town officer. He ignores us all as he strides to a nearby coffeemaker perched on top of some filing cabinets to get a refill.

The pretty brunette speaks up "Lieutenant, Mr. Grover's friends are here."

Hot Cop glances over his shoulder. "Fantastic. Mr. Grover, I'd really like not to see you in here for a while. Think that can be arranged?"

"We could arrange it easier if you'd agree to see me outside of the station, Lieutenant Haas. I'd love to help you celebrate that promotion of yours in style."

Hot Cop guy shakes his head as if he's lost all hope for the fate of humanity and points to the pretty offices Alonzo has been flirting with. "Owens, handle his paperwork and get him out of here."

The super-hot cop ambles over with his coffee, giving me and Ty an assessing look. "Listen, you two. If you're his friends, I'm hoping you guys might have enough pull to convince him to clean up his act. This isn't the first time we've caught him drunk or committing lewd acts in public. We've all got our troubles, but I looked the other way a few times in the past. Can't keep that up. It's gonna go downhill from here."

My gaze flies to meet Ty's. Too many questions jam in my throat, like why was Alonzo in such a rush to save my bacon when he clearly doesn't want to save his own, and what does this cop know about Alonzo's "troubles?"

There's no plane on which I can picture Alonzo coming clean to any kind of authority figure about his issues or his past. Yet the sympathy in Hot Cop's eyes tells me he must know something.

Not that I'm going to ask about that now. All that's coming out of me is a startled wheezing sound. Maybe that's good since I won't risk revealing the wrong thing.

Ty comes to, putting a surprisingly comforting hand on my shoulder. I can't tell him so, but it brings me back to the present and warms up my frozen lungs. "We'll do our best to keep an eye on him, officer," he says. "Thank you very much for your concern."

I never met Ty's grandmother before she died, but he says she made him study every morning and night, and wouldn't let him eat unless he said "please" and "thank you." I hear her in him every time he opens his mouth. He's always been the better of the two of us.

Maybe Terrence *was* right when he told me I'd never be good enough.

I clear my throat. "Yeah. We'll talk to him."

The officer nods and takes his coffee back to a desk, seating himself in front of a stack of paperwork. He goes back to ignoring us. We gather Alonzo and head outside.

"Okay. I am ready to find some breakfast." Stretching, I squint up at the sky. It's late morning by now and the sun's climbing overhead. Moreover, my stomach feels like it's eating itself

"Yeah, look guys," Alonzo mutters. "I'm still nursing a pretty shitty hangover. Maybe you two can go without me."

I look at Ty, who's only shaking his head. "No way," I tell Alonzo. "You owe me for coming to get your ass. I missed baked oatmeal for you."

Ty looks at me. "What the hell is baked oatmeal?"

"Damned if I know. Now I'm not going to find out now."

Alonzo leans into a large potted evergreen near the station steps and heaves the contents of his stomach. When he's done, he sags against the plant, no longer faking his flirty routine.

"Seriously, guys. I need to crash." He looks at Ty. "You've been jogging over every inch of Evergreen Grove. You can show her around. I'll owe you. Please?"

Ty rubs his face and I see him wanting to say no. I almost *want* him to say no. What would he and I do, spending time together? Pretend things are the way they used to be?

I also know there's too much guilt among us all, and we're trying hard to be normal. We're trying to be normal even though Alonzo hung over in the middle of a Tuesday morning and Ty without Terrance and me wanting to spend time with Ty almost as much as I want him to leave are *all* signs that nothing is normal and maybe never will be again.

People are so awful at accepting change, aren't they?

"Come on." Ty takes my hand and I don't know if he even realizes he has. "I'll give you the five-cent tour. We'll start with the really good bakery down on Main

Street. All kinds of muffins. Maybe it'll make up for your baked oatmeal."

I look back at Alonzo.

"Don't worry about me, boys and girls. I'll walk home. Fresh air'll do me good." He does still look rather green. Too bad, because his voice is a nice velvety brown.

Maybe the best way I can help Alonzo right now is to leave him alone. Or maybe it isn't, but I'm not sure what else to do. Shoe on the other foot, if he tried to give me some sanctimonious speech, I'd tell him to go fuck himself with a Juniper bush. He has to be tired of his own bullshit enough to do something different. Which is kind of how I'm feeling right now.

So I take a breath and look up at Ty. "All right, big guy. Feed me."

#

Ty - Then

After I told Kate she couldn't come to my fights anymore, I had to try to smooth things over. Trust me. That washed-out, wounded look on her face? Couldn't take the way that stuck in my chest.

So I made nice by agreeing to other, easier things. Things that seemed innocent. Like tagging along to help her pick up a used bookshelf she'd seen advertised in the local *Penny Pincher*—wasn't as if she could carry the thing herself. Or going along while she took photos for an art project. Wouldn't want her running around somewhere dangerous on her own, after all.

Maybe I was the last one to get the memo on how those excursions over time got to look a lot like dating. Especially when we'd stop at a diner for fried chicken on the way back or sit and talk in the sunshine for far too long.

Don't think it didn't occur to me that a nineteen year-old guy who threw down in a gravel lot as his primary source of income probably shouldn't be spending so much time with a girl busy trying to pass high school geometry.

Still. Every time she asked me to come along, I found excuses to say yes.

"So what is it with you and empty churches?"

She'd wanted to do this collage of abandoned houses of worship for her sociology class. Or some class. I couldn't remember. She'd explained one morning walking along some dried-up stretch of creek bed so she could take soil samples for science class, but I'd been distracted by making sure she didn't tumble on a loose rock.

There was always a project of some kind. That much I did know.

We had a lot of these little defunct churches around where we lived. Sitting there all forgotten in towns that weren't quite ghost towns, but that had fallen into such disrepair they might as well have been. Kate borrowed her mother's battered car one weekend and convinced me to ride along. So there we were, picking our way among a bunch of creepy-ass weathered gravestones.

"I think it's wondering whether or not anyone's home, you know? Like if the pastor and the worshippers leave, is God still in the house?" She'd lifted her camera and taken a picture of me standing in front of a dusty church with a busted sign that said, " ll welc m here."

"If my gran were alive she'd probably tell you God don't need a house to make a home."

She trained her camera on a pair of faded double doors. One falling off its hinges. "Is that what you believe?"

If that wasn't a huge question I didn't know what was. "I think it makes a certain amount of sense. Not that I was ever one for church, but the kind of faith my grandmother had was about praising good works and gathering with your friends for potato salad after. None of that required a particular building."

The way her face went dreamy and soft did something to my heart. "I love the way you talk about her. She must have been really special."

Now I was the one who probably had a dreamy smile. "She was. Took no lip. Loved harder than anyone. Terrence was born before midnight and me after, so every year she threw two separate parties on two separate days. Shortcake for Terrence. For me, sweet potato pie. She gave us everything she had and then some."

"That's amazing, Ty." For a second she lifted her camera again, but her hand wobbled and she let it down. Something about all that got to her. I stuffed my hands in my pockets, torn between changing the subject and putting a comforting arm around her, when she decided for me.

She cleared her throat and focused again on the small church, with its fading doors and peeling white paint. "Guess it's always been interesting to me. When my mom joined The Ministry of the Way and Light, it was about the minister. *His* supposed ability to channel God's healing power." She made a "talky, talky" gesture with her hand to show how much she believed in the teachings of her mother's church. "So by that theory, the minister goes, so does God?"

She tugged at a strand of her hair. "Or maybe God was never home and they were faking it like *The Wizard of Oz.*"

I laughed and shook my head. "You've thought about this more than I ever would."

"Product of growing up with my mom." There went that sad look again.

Not for the first time, I considered the differences in our upbringing. I'd had no mother or father thanks to the town drunk running them down one night while they were out walking. Happened only about a few months after Terrence and I were born, when Mom had asked Gran for a break from the stress of twins.

Still though. We'd had our gran, and until she'd died, life had been good.

Foster care had been a roller coaster. Some okay homes but more bad, and none lasted long as old as we were when we entered the system. The hardest part had been losing my bond with my twin. The one constant in my life, my best friend, ripped away. Not only physically.

Something changed in Terrence. He got distant and angry. I'd been trying to find ways to extend the olive branch, but things hadn't been the same.

Compare that to the fact that when Kate ripped her hand open tossing a tin can in the trash, she asked me to go with her to the clinic for stitches because her mother wouldn't have let her be treated. Man, I just don't know. At least for a while I knew I had a family I could count on.

I pointed to a gravestone. Some of them were practically my height and covered in line after line of faded writing. "These things are crazy."

"I know. What do you think they say?"

"Probably bible verses."

"Maybe it's like…stories."

"Stories."

"Yeah." She photographs some of the gravestones. "Or, like… The life and times of Bob Anderson, or whatever. 'Here lies Bob. He is survived by his wife, his mistress, and his dog Boomer, who all conspired to slowly sweeten his coffee with rat poison over French manicures once they found out he'd been stealing money and collectible Beanie Babies from them.'"

Ha. Sometimes she surprised the hell out of me. "Oh, yeah? Poor, stupid Bob."

"Poor Bob? Poor Boomer. Bob took his favorite dragon Beanie, and that one was really rare."

I shook my head. "I'm getting the scary feeling you secretly have a bunch of plastic-wrapped collectibles under your bed. And if you do, I don't want to know." I pointed to another headstone, getting into the game. "Look at this one here. At first you might think it's a passage from Thessalonians, but it's actually Mary Ruth's famous cookie recipe. She said she'd take it to her grave. She meant it literally."

She laughed such a carefree laugh I could only try to make it happen again.

I pointed to another. "And this one is just a really freaky poem about turtle sex."

That was exactly the wrong joke. It made her laugh out loud and squeeze in next to me, all warm and sweet-smelling. She leaned close and squinted, pretending to read the epitaph. "I can't quite read it. Which is too bad because now I'm dying to know what turtle sex is like."

"Slow."

Another burst of that musical sound broke the silence around us in that empty cemetery. Next thing I knew, her face was pressed right up right against mine.

At first, she only brushed her nose against my nose. The thick, warm afternoon air surrounded us and the high bushes near the church building rustled in the breeze. In spite of the solitude, I expected to be caught at any moment. Punished for kissing this girl.

After all, we were on holy ground. Weren't we?

Somewhere in the back of my head, I pondered Kate's earlier question about whether or not God was still home. Was he watching? Judging? Did he care?

But no punishment came. And kissing her tasted like both the brightest miracle and the sweetest sin. Softest lips I'd ever tasted. Warm tongue. A little hint of the chocolate chip muffins she'd brought for a snack that day.

Then she'd said four little words to strike fear in my heart:

"My parents aren't home."

In my guts I knew we weren't there yet. I wasn't. Not yet. Not with this girl.

"You know, I think it's time for us to head back," I'd said to Kate with my hand on her chin. She'd lifted up on her toes like she wanted another kiss.

I'd wanted to give it to her. I'd wanted to give her everything. As much as I loved the warmth curling in my gut from the way her tongue had stroked along mine, the place and time wasn't right.

"Ty. You could come over," she'd said. "My mom has a church thing tonight, and my dad's visiting his mother in Virginia."

Right. I'd reminded her firmly of our age difference again. She'd pouted, and having kissed her now, that did almost sway me. Two and a half years didn't seem like so much. Until you considered that she wasn't yet eighteen.

"The age of consent is sixteen in South Carolina, Ty. I looked it up. You wouldn't get in any kind of trouble."

Here we were, standing in a church. Arguing about sex. Couldn't help but think I was being tested.

"Not getting in trouble shouldn't be where we set the bar. When we're together it should be the right time. Not just because we jumped at the first opportunity."

My grandmother had talked about how sex was better when the person you were with was right. Right time, right place. Her version of sex ed. included honoring sex as a spiritual commitment. Not saying I hadn't blown off that rule early on thanks to easy access and raging hormones. With Kate, I wanted things to be different. I wanted everything to be perfect.

She gave me a teasing smile. "Who said I want to have sex? Maybe I want you to come over to see my stamp collection."

"You've got a stamp collection? You keep that with the Beanie Babies?"

"I *could* have a stamp collection."

"Something tells me you haven't got the patience for tiny, sticky pieces of paper that have to be handled with a magnifying glass and Tweezers."

Her lips form something between a pout a smile. "I have an idea. Senior prom. It's five days before my eighteenth birthday. That's special. And maybe more… Uh, better. Timing, I mean. For you."

Senior prom. No way did I want to get dressed up in some damn monkey suit and go drink punch in a high school gym.

So much would be easier if I could bring myself to walk away from this girl. Except I'd learned from life that people who honestly cared about you didn't come by the dozen.

And there she was, still staring. Still smiling. Waiting for an answer. Hopeful. Those wide, dark eyes. How the hell does a guy say no to those wet eyelashes?

"Senior prom's over a year away. Who says you'll still want me around by then?"

"I will. You'll see."

With one more touch of her long, dark hair, I'd given in. "Okay then. I guess we'll see."

I'd held out that carrot, thinking the day would never come. Except it came all right. Just ended in our worst nightmares.

9. ALL THE BAKERIES IN ALL THE SMALL TOWNS

"What are we doing, Ty?" She asks me this as I hold out a muffin and coffee.

"The answer isn't obvious?" I know she's got a head injury and all, but coffee and a muffin at breakfast should pretty much explain itself.

She gives me a look like I'm the one with the head injury. "I mean, you could've taken me back to the B&B. Whatever you told Alonzo, it's not your job to show me around Evergreen Grove. The lady that runs the inn can tell me all about where to find things in town. Hell, I can go ask the mailman. He seems friendly."

To make her point, she gives a wave to old Walt, who's going past the window of the bakery. The man smiles and waves back, because that's how people are around here. Stops to talk as he passes folks.

Even so, the idea of Mr. McFeely giving my Kate the town tour makes my jaw tight.

"First," I plunk down the cranberry muffin I got for her, "eat your muffin. Second, we're here because you agreed to it, too, so we're gonna keep on with the plan. Third, when you called all frantic about helping Alonzo, I borrowed someone's car and he owns the gym across the street. If nothing else, I need to return the man's vehicle."

I point over to where I've parked Dante's Jeep in front of Delia's, and the big man who's heading over from the gym as we speak. When the frantic phone call came through, I'd asked him for info on getting to the sheriff's station, and he'd made the surprisingly generous offer. Surprising until he grinned and said, "We can talk more when you bring my ride back."

This is how friendly folks get you in small towns.

Kate stares me down, not looking particularly placated. With a jerky thrust that almost topples both our coffees, she shoves the muffin and coffee back to my side of the table. "I don't like cranberry anymore. Or coffee." Her confusion and frustration would appear to match my own. I'm about to ask her about it when her eyes soften and she slips out a grudging, "Thank you, though. For getting them."

With that, she leaves me alone at the table to go and order herself something else. Shoulda let her do that from the jump, I guess. Keep thinking I still know her. Maybe I'm only wishing I did.

"There he is. That was quick." Dante's smiling at me when I look up again.

I do my best to smile back. Usually friendly is my default mode. With Kate around to twist me in knots, I'm struggling now to drum it up.

"Yeah. Thanks for the loaner. No worries, your baby's back safe."

That earns me a hearty laugh. "My baby's name is Michelle, and I don't loan her out. Still though, I appreciate you got my ride back safe. Your friend okay?"

Before I can think better of keeping my business under wraps, I frown and shrug my shoulders. Trouble is, I've wondered for months if Alonzo's bought himself a ticket on a slow cruise to destruction and I can't figure out how to help him get off the ride.

"Not so okay?"

I glance back at Dante. "Oh. Sorry. He's okay, I guess. Kinda one of those people who keeps getting himself into trouble."

Dante licks his lip. "Got it. I used to be one of those people. Not another casualty of Arlo Specter, I hope?"

My fingers drum on the table, almost without my permission. "I guess you could say he wasn't at ground zero, but he got tagged by flying shrapnel."

Dante rubs his chin. "That's rough. Hope one of these days we can make that fucker pay for what he's done."

I know what he's telling me. "Same here. Though I'm worried what I know won't help you. I overheard some things, but I don't think I have what would be called solid proof."

"Never hurts to try."

Except sometimes trying kills you. If I can't tell this guy the truth, then Terrence's death might have been for nothing. But if I do tell him, it might be the thing that kills me for good.

"What are we trying?" Kate's back with her new bakery choices.

"Cranberry muffin, apparently." Biting the one she rejected, I give Kate a look as she sits across from me with…looks like a banana muffin and hot cocoa. Extra whipped cream.

Mature as ever, she responds by sticking out her tongue. More actually mature, she turns to Dante and offers a hand. "Kate."

"Dante Ramos. Nice to meet you."

"Ohmygod. I saw you on TV…" A dark flush rises to her cheeks. "Wow. Of all the bakeries in all the small towns."

She likes him. Of course she does. Rumor has it Dante was one hell of a smooth operator back in the day. Guess having a steady woman in his life can't stop the ladies from wanting him.

And Kate's not mine. Never really was, because I was stupid enough not to publicly claim her. So it makes no difference to me if a girl I never even officially dated wants to bat her lashes at this guy. No difference at all.

Except right now seeing her shake his hand and smile up into his face so openly—so different from the careful, curious way she looks at me—I can't sit here and watch. "Okay, so good talking to you, man. Promised Kate here I'd show her around town, though, so we'd better be on our way."

Did that sound as bad as I think it did?

Kate's giving me the evil eyes. So maybe. "Kinda wanted to finish my cocoa, Ty."

"We'll drive while we walk. It'll keep you warm."

"But I got a spoon so I can eat the whipped cream off the top."

Damn, she's good.

Dante seems unfazed. "Oh, cool. New to the area? Be sure to check out the falls. Great camping and hiking year round if you're not afraid of a little cold, and then there's the Heart and Hearth for a nice dinner out, that little art gallery up on The Ridge, and of course one town over we've got a college campus with all sorts of stuff to do. Great little park down the road. All sorts of shopping. Definitely stop in the gym and I'll hook you up with a guest membership. Where you staying?"

"Oh. The bed and breakfast for now, but I could use a more permanent option. Do you know of any apartments or houses for rent?"

He strokes his chin. "Hmm. There's a single apartment building in Evergreen Grove. Over in the direction of the college campus. Sometimes people put houses up for rent. You might check the bulletin board here or over at the church." He points to the wall at the back of Delia's, next to a counter full of milk pitchers and sugar packets, where people have posted "lost dog" and "car for sale" ads.

"You'll have more luck if you look over by the college campus. You can rent a portion of a large apartment instead of a whole one or two bedroom. Oh. My fiancée's buddy might be moving out of his place. I can give her a call."

Is it me or does Kate look disappointed at the mention of *fiancée?* "Sure," she says. "Thanks."

"You bet." He gives her his card. Same one he gave me, but still. Is he just handing those babies out like candy? "Let me know if you need any help. You two have a great day. And Tyler, I'll be seeing you later to discuss your class, right?"

"Yeah. Thanks." Fan-flipping-tastic. Pretty sure I officially said yes to that kiddie class. I grab her hand. "Come on. Let's go find you a place to live."

"What? Now? Seriously?"

"You seriously think you're gonna be staying in town?"

"Well." All of a sudden, her face falls. "I tried to call my mom yesterday. To smooth things over. She told me I was ruining her life. Hers. We got into a shouting match and I hung up on her. So yeah, I guess I'm kind of hoping staying here for awhile works out because I don't know where else I might go. I had one bridge and I burned it, Ty."

I'm not even sure when I grabbed her hand, but I'm wrapping my fingers around hers, reacquainting myself with the smoothness of her palm. "Okay. Then let's seriously find you a place to call home."

Kate's mother will have to take care of her own life choices. What I *can* do is fix Kate's living situation. And something in me can't let some other big shot be the guy who helps her solve this one.

I need to be the one who's there for her. This time, I'm damn well going to be.

#

Kate

I don't know what surprises me more. The fact that Ty's suddenly all over the idea of helping me out, or that he honestly seems sincere about it.

The things he said after I woke up in the hospital, they make my insides cold every time I think about them.

I've missed the guy who used to walk me home in the evenings. You wouldn't believe how many fake research projects I came up with so I could go to the library even more often. It got so ridiculous I was asking friends in other grades about their homework for good material.

As we make our way slowly along the brick streets of Evergreen Grove, I almost feel like we're back, you know, *before.* The chill pushing us close. The uneven brick pavement has me choosing my steps carefully, and him watchful in case I land on my face. All the same, it's nice.

"You okay to walk? There's supposed to be a local bus. I could get a schedule."

"Oh God, no. Buses are bumpy. Worse than being a passenger in a car. I'm good walking, so long as we take it slow."

He eyeballs me a little too hard. There were times when I loved his height and his muscles and the intensity of his presence. Now isn't one of those times. "So if you don't like cars or public transportation, how the hell you get around?"

"Honestly, I don't go out a lot. Why do you think I've stayed living with my mom all this time? When I do go, muscle relaxers help."

"Be serious."

"I am." Sadly.

"That what I saw you trying to buy off that girl the night Alonzo and I picked you up?"

I shrug. "The doctor I've been seeing gave me valium and stuff, but I'm on my last refill. Hey, look. I think that's the park your friend mentioned." I point across the street to an expanse of grass with some guys in the high school and twenty-something range playing a casual game of tackle football in spite of the cold.

When I turn back, Ty has his mad face on and he's giving me one mother of a stare down. "Okay, just don't. Okay? I don't need your judgment. You don't know what this has been like for me."

"I don't need to know what it's been like for you to know that you're on a fast track to addiction once you start buying your pharmaceuticals without a prescription."

He's not wrong. I've tried to be careful. I've spaced out my medication. I've taken half doses and split pills to ensure I didn't numb out too much, but stopping entirely is hard. Hard when every time you're awake you feel pain, and harder when that pain keeps you from sleeping.

With a racing heart, I turn and head away from him. A bitter wind picks up and a pile of dead leaves smack me in the face. "Oh. Great. Lovely. Look," I say as I turn back again. "Remember when I said no judgment?"

"Not judging a thing." He shakes his head. "What I'm doing is stating a fact. You know how many out-of-work guys back in Aspiration had pill habits. You need more meds than the doctor can give you? It's a problem."

I don't realize I'm crying until another burst of wind hits my cheek and the freeze is extra cold. "Ty, I don't want to hurt all the time. That's all."

"Hey." This time he sounds kind when he speaks. He draws me close, placing his hand on the back of my neck. "What's the problem, exactly?"

I look up at the sky. It's a pretty blue-gray morning, not super sunny but clear. When his thumb brushes a stray tear from my cheek, I look up to see the gentlest smile on his face.

"You mean, physically?"

"Physically. I may not be a doctor, but I know my way around the human body."

Some part of me wants to push aside all this painful emotion and say something flirty. I mean, come on. The door for that joke was left wide open. The way Ty's being sweet to me though, I don't want to go spooking him.

So I tell him the truth. "There aren't too many places it doesn't hurt. I mean, aside from the headaches, it's kind of a constant in my neck and shoulder, and then my back hurts a lot. Mostly my lower back. Sometimes my hips. And that… Ugh. That thing in the top of my leg that gets squished when my butt muscles are too tight."

"Sciatic nerve."

"God bless you." I know what it's called, but that thing happened again. My brain glitched and I couldn't find the word.

He gives me an impatient look. "You mind if I touch you?"

I've been waiting years for him to touch me. This isn't at all how I'd hoped it'd go down. "Do whatever you need to do."

His fingers walk along the back of my neck. God, his hands are huge. So warm and firm. I want to melt into his touch, and I can literally feel the knots of my muscles unraveling under his hands.

"I think I know what you need."

A puff of steamy breath floats from his mouth to my ear, and when I shiver I don't think it's from the cold. I think I know what I need, too. Probably isn't the thing he's thinking.

Wishing to hide his effect on me, I look up to his face and give him a skeptical lift of my eyebrow. "Oh yeah? You've got two male models and a heated massage table handy?"

He grunts and comes around behind me, pressing close while his hands run down my back. Up underneath my jacket. Another shiver when he lifts the hem to expose my back to cold air, but immediately his big hands are there to cover me, running up the length of my spine.

"Your muscles are all knotted up. They're hard and tight, but you don't have a lot of tone."

I've had a dozen physical therapists say those words or something quite similar, and it never sounded exactly that way. Not so…suggestive.

"You caught me." I turn to face him, cold again without his hands on my skin. "They're hard because I'm the woman of steel. It's my super-secret superhero identity. I've come to this small town to keep it safe from villains with names like 'Green Goober' and 'Persnickety Platypus'."

"Oh yeah? I saw him last week. Seemed like an okay dude. Funny looking, but cool."

I try not to laugh, but it comes out anyway. Actually, it sounds quite suspiciously like a girlish giggle. This is going to do nothing for my superhero image.

I lift my chin and clear my throat. "Uh-huh. So. What is it you think I need?"

"Seriously though, your muscles are weak so I think they're straining harder than they need to, which is causing you pain. Your PT ever have you do any strength training?"

"Sure. Some." When I went to my appointments, which I stopped doing a while ago. Yes, I was supposed to continue the exercises. No, I didn't really. I was depressed and exhausted, and taking pain meds was way easier. At first, anyway.

"My bet…" He hesitates, a cloud of emotion coming over his face. I can see that he's thinking about the accident. It was bound to happen, what with us talking about my injury. I hate that pain on his face all the same.

Maybe this is the real reason we haven't kept in touch. He didn't want me to remind him.

He swallows hard and then coughs before continuing. "My bet is every muscle in your body went tight when you had that wreck. To try and protect your injuries. So now your muscles are weak from disuse—lying around let them heal but also let them get soft after too long. So when you experience hurt your body tries to tighten and protect your injury like before, only now your muscles are weak—"

"It's painful to exercise. And I'm tired a lot. Still."

"I'm sure you are. But see, it's created a vicious cycle. If you got yourself stronger, physically, your muscles wouldn't need to fight so hard to hold your joints and everything steady. They wouldn't feel so sore all the time."

I mull over his assessment. "I guess it makes sense. I wonder why nobody ever explained it to me that way. I might've done the exercises more if they had. It never felt like they were doing much good."

He shrugs and turns his face away. "I don't know, Kate. Everything I know about anatomy and physiology I picked up in a gym. Those PTs and doctors have real medical training. I'm only telling you what makes sense to me. You won't hurt so much if your body is stronger. When was the last time you worked out?"

He's got me there. "Aside from PT? I seem to recall watching you fight got my heart rate up back in the day. Does that count?"

His scowl tells me he does not find this funny.

"Oh, come on. My wrist sets off the metal detector at the county courthouse, for crying out loud. You know I'm not exactly in fighting shape, here."

"We can start you off easy. Dante said he'd give you a trial membership at the gym. Somehow I agreed to teach a martial arts class for kids, so I'll be over there plenty anyway. I can help you come up with a plan. Light weights, cardio and stretching. Work your muscles back up again, and I'm betting you that constant achiness will go away."

"Oh, yeah? If we're betting things, what do I get if you're wrong?"

His cocky smile returns. "Well, either way you win, right? You'll be in better shape."

I roll my eyes. Can't help it. "Geez, Ty. If I wanted to be told what was good for me, I could have stayed living with my mom."

"I'm not throwing you over my shoulder and hauling you to church. I'm offering help that will have measurable results."

I roll my eyes again. Yes, my mother did physically drag me to church once when I didn't want to go. Yes, it's on my list of issues.

He states his case again. "Look, do it for Alonzo. Do it for me. I lost Terrence, and if I lose you to some pill habit after almost losing you before, I won't know how to be okay."

Ouch. "Fine. I'll try. But if I do, you think you could try and forgive me?"

He frowns at me, looking honestly confused. "Forgive you?"

Does he not remember what he said? I take a step back, chickening out because, well, what if? If I push this button and force the question of whether or not he still blames me for Terrence's death, do I really want to hear him say the answer is yes?

No. I don't.

Not when this is already the best day I've had since I woke up in the hospital asking to die.

10. A LOT LIKE HAPPINESS

The apartment place Dante pointed us to is a great one for Kate. A small building full of one-bedroom units on the edge of Evergreen Grove, only a handful of blocks from Alonzo's house. I'm sure I've passed it a dozen times while jogging and not noticed.

Due to the size of the units, mostly it's full of grad students or the few young singles who live in Evergreen Grove. Kate would have the quiet she says she needs. Most of the places closer to campus are two- and four-bedroom places with lots of parties.

Still, I know we're in trouble when she comes out of the manager's unit with moisture-rimmed eyes, and I know I'm gonna regret asking. But I do. "What's wrong?"

"He's got one unit open. I can afford it, but he wants a pay stub. I haven't had a job recently because of..."

She doesn't finish, but she rubs this one spot over her eyebrow. I've seen her do it before, whether she meant to or not. It must be some kind of nervous habit. Maybe a sign of a headache? The only time I managed to see her in the hospital, that part of her head was covered in bandages.

"Don't worry, it's not as bad as looks," the nurse who'd snuck me into the room had said.

Found out later she'd had a fractured skull. Sounds to me like it was exactly as bad as it looked. She'd been asleep, knocked out on the pain meds probably, so I'd had no choice but to vent my anguish and disappear before her parents showed up.

Just before walking out of the room, I swore she'd opened her eyes. An involuntary reflex, the nurse told me. Still, leaving her in that room to go and lay my brother to rest nearly killed me.

Don't handle seeing pain in her eyes any better now than I did then. "Let's see what we can do to work this out," I say as I wrap an arm around her shoulder. Try to tell myself her body doesn't fit perfectly against mine, tucked up under my arm.

"I can look on campus like your friend Dante mentioned." I go stiff when she mentions Dante. I don't need to be bothered that she's talking about him. Not even if Dante wasn't engaged. Which he is. Not that I care either way.

Still though.

"You said you don't like noise. The campus apartments are party central. Plus it'll be hard to find something this time of year." I give her a nudge. "I think Ethan and his girl will be moving out of Alonzo's before too long. He's got his own room. Might be quieter than the others over there."

She shakes her head and I pretend not to notice when she wipes away a tear. "It's too much. I get headaches, and too much noise, it gets chaotic. I don't sleep well as it is."

"But you don't mind the noise from a band."

"Music isn't chaos, Ty. Music is poetry." Her pronouncement might sound stuck-up if it wasn't followed by a quiet sniffle and a careful swipe at her nose from the napkin she took from the café.

I can't fight all that. Crying women aren't something I'm equipped to withstand, at least not this one.

Show me a man who is and I'll show you a dude with a problem. "All right. Let me handle this."

My fist lands heavily on the manager's door. I want him to know the person on the other side isn't playing.

"Yeah?" He's an older guy. Pasty yellow-white skin with a pink scalp and a mustache that looks like bristles from the toothbrush I recently tossed in the trash. After I used it to clean the bathroom tile. Dingy and tired-looking. More or less what I expected from a guy who fleeces students for money.

While Kate was looking at the apartment, I'd stayed out of the way. This was her thing and I didn't want to get into the middle. Didn't want to give the picture to anyone, least of all me, that we were together. If this guy's denying Kate a place to live though, I have to take a different approach.

"Hello, sir." Gran always insisted we be respectful to our elders. Even old men whose gin-blossomed noses suggested diminished capacity. "I'm Kate's…friend. She said there's a problem with her application."

He holds up his hands as if he's helpless. "Look. I need some kinda proof of being able to pay the damn rent. She's got no pay stub, no references, no nothing."

Behind me, she sniffles again. "I told you, I have plenty in savings."

"Yeah, and I have a rare baseball card collection, but I can't use it to pay for my mother's foot amputation."

"Okay, hold up." I chew on the fact that I'm about to get myself more deeply rooted in a town where I never meant to take up permanent residence. Looking back at Kate, I ask, "You sure this is where you want to stay?"

She chews her lip. "It's a nice apartment. I can find something else though, Ty. It's okay."

She likes the apartment. I'll get her the damn apartment. "Okay, so you know Dante Ramos? Down at the gym?"

Guy chuckles. "Everyone knows Dante."

"Right." They used to air his fights on Pay-Per-View after all. "So I work for Dante at the gym. You can call down there and get him to verify, if you want. I could cosign the lease, right? Between her bank account and my gainful employment, would that put your mind at ease, sir?"

He leans against the doorframe in an ugly-ass orange sweater, squinting and rubbing his chin. I hate the way he's sizing me up. Maybe it's too much time spent in foster homes, too much time getting appraised for my size or my clothes or any number of reasons, but it's hard not to wonder if I'm being evaluated and found lacking.

Behind me, Kate's gripping my biceps with nails I wish she'd trim. Except I'm standing between her and something she needs. That fills me with power and presses my lungs flat all at once. What is it about this girl that's always made me think I'm the biggest man on earth and about to mess something up at the same time?

Finally, the building manager deigns to give us more information. "Fine. Place needs some plumbing work. Might take a couple of weeks. If you're willing to wait, we can work something out."

Kate's bouncing on the balls of her feet. "It's okay. I can wait."

God help the girl if she ever has to negotiate for a used car. *That's okay, I don't need a discount. While we're at it, why don't I just go ahead and write you a check now for the extended warranty, rust protection, and glow-in-the-dark squid insurance? Sounds legit.*

Landlord hands over some papers. "You put your info down on the application, she can have the place. I'll call Ramos to verify your employment, like you said. Make sure you include address and phone number." He glances between us. "Less you'll be living here."

Whoa. Yeah. Not touching that statement.

Turns out I don't have to. Before I have the time to think about it, Kate comes around and launches herself into my arms. "Oh my God, thank you. I can't even believe you would do that for me. Thankyouthankyouthankyou."

I look at her, inches from my face, eyes sparkling with something that looks a hell of a lot like happiness. "I can't believe you jumped into my arms. It didn't hurt your back?"

"Oh." She laughs. "Wow. You're right. I totally did. I was so excited, I didn't even think."

Hard not to go to all sorts of places where you get a girl so excited, she jumps you without thinking. "Well, see. You jumped and you're okay. Maybe if you don't worry so much about hurting yourself all the time, you won't need so many of those pills."

That last part I say with a laugh, so she won't take it as judgment. I also ease her down to the floor so she can get away from me in case she does. She stops halfway, our faces right in front of each other. Or I stop. Not really sure who's doing this, now that I think harder about it.

I'm only sure about the way she's looking at me. The way her lips are dark pink and thick and soft looking. The way I can't stop myself when she licks her bottom lip and tips her head.

The second our lips brush I'm back home. I'm feeling keyed-up and forbidden and wildly turned on all at the same time. Humming with adrenaline the way I do before a fight.

The good guy in me always wanted to wait until she was older. We're both older now.

"Ahem."

But apparently no wiser.

One brush of her lips. One gentle swipe of her tongue. That's all I get before her new smug-looking landlord shoves a handful of papers between us.

"Forgot to give you the credit check forms. You lovebirds can go ahead and give these back when you're finished filling them out. I'll also be needing one month's deposit."

She grabs the papers and I take a pen too quickly, scrawling a jagged black line across my palm. Neither of us speak for the next twenty minutes, except for when she asks me to swap pens because hers is out of ink.

#

Ty

The sun is rising again in Evergreen Grove. Again, I'm jogging to clear my head.

Yesterday was pretty much a bust after managing to get Kate her apartment. Still not sure how I let things get so out of control. Maybe Alonzo was right though. Things weren't the same without her around.

My emotions are all twisted since the kiss. Really, I've been twisted since the first time she kissed me, just shy of her seventeenth birthday. Since it felt completely wrong and completely right all at the same time. Felt the same way yesterday, even though we're both plenty old enough. Still can't help but wonder if she and I are just always doomed to wrong-place-wrong-time situations. Or right-place-wrong-time ones, maybe.

I put my face into the wind and let the cold air burning my nostrils, the sting of it on my face, take over. I pound the concrete with shoes that should've been replaced months ago. All these sensations are easier, better things to focus on than the way putting my lips on Kate's has invaded every inch of free space in my brain.

Times like these, I miss my brother the most. If he were here, I'd have someone I could talk all this out with. Someone to help me get my life back on track like a grown-ass adult. Then again, Terrence didn't have much good to say about Kate toward the end. Hard to know what he'd say now.

Once again I don't realize I'm coming up on the gym until the door opens and smiling Dante Ramos steps out. Damn.

"Hey, if it isn't my newest employee. Great to see you're on time."

Funny. I know what I said to Kate's knew landlord, but I didn't actually talk to Dante about showing up anywhere at a particular time. Doesn't seem like the thing to say though.

When I reach the former heavyweight champ, I pull up short. "Yeah. Hey. Morning."

He's the last person I want to see in my current mood. Still though, I sort of screwed myself.

"So I got a phone call yesterday afternoon. Guess you're definitely on tap for that class."

Yeah, that'd be the way. "Guess so."

"Something change your mind?"

"Had to help out a friend." I shrug my shoulders and pretend to be looking around, up and down Main Street. I'm not great at lying. Also, what I did for Kate, I wouldn't have done for most people. "Anyway, it could be fun. Teaching kids."

Fun. Bowel-shaking. For some people they're practically the same.

"I gotcha." Dante leans back against the brick front of his gym. "And by friend, do you mean that pretty young 'it's complicated' friend who was having breakfast with you yesterday morning?"

I rub the back of my neck and study the gym equipment that I can see through the door. Didn't look around a whole lot when I was here before. It's actually a pretty nice place. Small, but well-equipped. Clean. There's a practice ring, heavy bag, some weight equipment and a couple of bikes and treadmills. Nobody inside yet this early, except the one guy I met before who said his daughter wanted to take my class.

Dante gives me a firm tap on the shoulder. "I hear you loud and clear, buddy."

"You do?" Funny since I didn't say a damn word.

"Listen, since you'll be working here, you may as well come in and get started. Get back in the ring. Start training again. Be good for you to take another swing at a pro career."

Dangerous, painful hope hits me right in my center. "I don't think so."

"You don't want to? Because I see scraped knuckles and some facial bruising that tells me you've been fighting. Might as well get back in business and try to get paid."

I scratch the back of my head. “Look, that’s cool of you, but I already blew my shot at the big time. There’s no going back.”

“Says who?”

You screw this up and you’ll never fight again. I’ll make sure you don’t.

Arlo Specter, for one. “Everyone in the business saw me blow that fight against ZZ Marques, and I’m out of practice. A street fight against a college punk with money to blow is different. People aren’t exactly lining up to give me second chances. Probably too old now anyway.”

Dante heads in, over to the practice ring. “Too old.” He makes a dismissive noise. “This ain’t ballet, man.” He points over to where that guy AJ is hitting the heavy bag. “AJ’s boyfriend’s ex is a ballerina. You know you gotta be on the career track by fucking elementary school or you’re royally screwed?

“Fighter’s *shouldn’t* start that early. Arlo Specter feed you that line of bullshit? Sick piece of shit liked to get kids started young. Tried to convince them they’d be nothing if he didn’t take ’em under his wing. Fact is, you can’t fight professional until age eighteen anyway, and plenty of professional fighters started in their mid-twenties. You’re still practically in diapers where your career is concerned.”

I snort like he’s full of it, but I’m forced to admit he has a decent point. Here I am not yet twenty-five and feeling like it’s way past too late. In my head I know a lot of fighters out there are older. In my gut? I wonder if I’ve taken too many wrong turns.

“Guess I figured if I blew that first fight so badly, I wasn’t about to get another try. You know.”

"Yeah, except I saw the film of that match. Didn't look like having skills was the problem. My hard-earned money says you had a reason for losing that fight. And it wasn't because you couldn't win."

I did. I lost on purpose. Which was something so unthinkable I'd tried to block out the fact until now. Stated so boldly, with no room for question or argument in Dante's tone, I have no choice but to face the truth. "I *had* to lose that fight."

"Come here." Dante tosses me some practice equipment and climbs into the center of the ring. I'm grateful for the distraction as I pull on gloves and head-gear.

We face off in the center, me slightly taller and Dante slightly broader, and go to town. My mistake is thinking that Dante was a boxer, so of course he wouldn't be so experienced with other fighting techniques.

That's what I think right before a leg sweep knocks me to the floor.

I spit out my mouth guard. "Ow. Damn."

"Someone needs another cup of coffee."

I laugh and accept the hand he holds out. "Yeah. Maybe I would've been prepared if I'd known—"

"You should always be prepared. So'd Arlo make you throw the fight?"

The back of my neck gets hot. Tight. "Not the way you think. He wanted me to win. I decided not to."

Dante squares up with me. "Ok. Let me see what else you got, kid."

We shove in our mouth guards and face off again. This time I dodge when he comes at me and take a swing, which he blocks.

"You're fast," he mumbles.

I shrug.

We trade a few more jabs. I duck his punches pretty easily, but he's quick on his feet. Spinning me in circles. Soon as I figure out his game, I switch up my tactic, pressing him backward into the ropes.

Without warning, he drops his arms and sways on his feet. Maybe he's sick or something? I'd think he's about to pass out or whatever except I only got a couple of body blows in and they weren't hard hits.

"Hey, man, are you okay—"

Dante's fist shoots out, stopping just under the soft portion of my jaw. "Gotcha." He laughs, but it's more of a friendly laugh than a hey-I-kicked-your-ass laugh.

"You've got potential," he says again after we've quit. "You're fast, you're a southpaw, and you've got talent. It's a good combo."

"Thanks." I lean back against the ropes, unsure about his sincerity. "That was a nice fake-out."

"What you see is not always what is. And I mean it. You're good." He climbs down out of the ring to grab a bottle of water and hands one over.

"Sure. Thanks."

He leans next to me, staring off in thought. "So I still have contacts in the business. Fight promoters who wouldn't whiz on Specter even for funzies. Maybe I could hook you up."

"No. No thank you. If I get back into the game, I feel like it's something I ought to do on my own."

He looks at me with narrowed eyes. "It's a lot of maybes. You fight your ass off in tiny venues, maybe if you're lucky you get picked up by bigger guys. Maybe you hit the big time and become one of the guys they're booking slots on paid cable for. Or maybe you wind up making four grand a year and spending double that in medical bills. I'm only offering to put in a good word."

My chest burns. I appreciate what he's offering, but… "I just can't live with feeling like I traded my success for my brother's pain."

Dante's still and silent now, regarding me with eyes that know way too much. I hate knowing that it's all happened to him, and right about now I mostly hate it because he knows exactly what I'm saying about Terrence.

I couldn't save my brother. And he knows that, too.

"So that's why you threw the fight."

"I don't know the whole story. I do know Specter agreed to hook me up with a high profile fight. They made some kind of deal. Arlo Specter got me on the ticket with Marques. Terrence paid him some kind of…favors."

Just like that I'm gagging, lurching. At the memory of what I saw, what I heard.

I'm fighting with myself on the inside. Cold. Pissed. Shivering and angry. I hate Dante Ramos of all people seeing me this way and I want to punch him in that pretty face for making me say what I just said out loud.

Before my anger has a chance to boil into rage, a large plastic bucket is in my hands.

"Here. In case you need to hurl."

"Nah. I think I'm good." Actually, I can't be sure. Puking in front of someone I admire isn't something I'm willing to do, though. I take some deep breaths and wait for the feeling to pass. Still sick, but calmer.

He rubs a hand across his forehead. "Look. I know all of Specter's bullshit. My ma, she had medical bills. He paid them and I was stuck owing. That was his leverage with me. In your case, your brother wanted to help your career, I guess."

I shake my head. "I don't know. I get the feeling it went on longer than that, but I do know for sure Arlo guaranteed Terrence a match-up that would get me attention."

Sad and humiliating at the same time.

Dante stands and offers me a hand up. "Yeah. He used people's weaknesses. Often family. So fuck him, right? He sets up a fight for you and you blow it on purpose?"

"That's pretty much the size of it. Yeah."

Dante's smile is slow, but his laugh is a burst of sound. "That's fucking great. Good for you. Wish I'd done that a hell of a lot sooner."

I almost laugh. Me, I wish I'd done a lot of things differently. "Thanks. Still though, I know you're looking for more information for your case against Specter. I want to help but I don't know if I can."

"We can always help each other. Maybe you talk to the DA. Maybe you don't. Maybe you can help the case, maybe you can't. Maybe none of the above but at least I've got a new employee, maybe even a friend. Can't have too many friends in a small town like Evergreen Grove."

I accept his handshake of agreement. I definitely wouldn't mind having another friend in town.

11. NAUSEATINGLY WRONG

Ty - Then

"What in the hell was that?"

After losing against ZZ Marques, all I wanted was to be alone. Terrence found me in the locker room. I had a towel around my waist, one over my head, and a piece of rolled-up gauze in my nostril to stop the bleeding from my nose.

My body hurt like it'd been run through the cleaners. Last thing I needed was my brother giving me trouble. "Told you I didn't want to take that fight."

He hit his hand against an open locker. The force slammed it closed with an unholy clang of metal that did nothing for my aching head. "So you decided to lie down and take the loss? He was a champion moving up from another weight class Ty, but you had him on size. No way you didn't have him beat."

"What can I say? Dude was scrappy."

It took fierce effort just to lift my shoulders in a shrug. Beyond the hurt, I was bone-tired. All I wanted was to wait for the fans and TV people to clear out of the halls out there so I could go back to where I was crashing on my friend's sofa and sleep forever.

"That's all you've got? Are you serious with this? Is that *all* you've got after what I did to get you here?" Terrence descended on me with his wrath flying high.

"I didn't want you to pull strings for me!" I stood so fast I knocked him back. "You should've asked me before you made a deal with some sick old white dude.

There is no way I'm doing a thing that man tells me to, and I can't see why *you* would!"

Terrence's face twisted. "He isn't all bad. He's gotten me fair contracts and good fights. You hear about fighters getting in the ring because all they want is to make a name, and instead they get beaten to death and paid nothing because nobody was looking out for them. He looks out for me, Tyler. *And* he helped get your name on the radar of some of his contacts in UFC."

Dammit. I hated myself then for not knowing Terrence needed someone to handle those things for him. For not being able to be that person. I hated Arlo Specter more for using my brother's need for a father figure for his own twisted gain.

"You and I, we could have made our own way. We still can. I won't let him use you anymore."

Terrence looked away. He had his arms wrapped around himself, his hands holding his elbows. For the first time in years, vulnerability seeped through the cracks in his angry mask.

If there was ever a time to let on that I knew exactly what had been going on between my brother and Arlo Specter, that was the moment. But I told myself Terrence deserved his privacy.

So all I said was, "I don't want to see you get hurt, Terrence."

"I'm okay."

But are you, though? Really? How can you possibly be?

Still, he bounced back quickly. "Look, it's all good. We'll fix this. We'll apologize to Arlo. He can set you up another gig and this time—"

I pushed the towel back from my head so he could see me when I said, "Terrence, stop."

He did. Arms mid-gesture and everything. His expression told me he already knew.

"You remember that time Granny chased off those kids on the corner who were throwing rocks at a stray dog? She said even animals deserve basic kindness."

He rolled his eyes but reluctantly confessed to the memory. "Yeah. So?"

"So before the fight started, he was already talking about more. The next fight. The next promo. Some damn camera crew he'd sent out to our old house to capture the shithole we grew up in. He wasn't going to let it rest until he'd turned our private lives inside-out."

A muscle ticked in my brother's jaw. "Lots of fighters do promo, T. It's how they make their money."

"Brother, he was signing me on for things I never agreed to. I'm not gonna let a bunch of people with cameras follow me around, the poor charity case supposedly helped out, so he can pretend to be some kind of hero."

Terrence's jaw hardened. Noteworthy though that he didn't look so surprised. I knew then that something between us was broken. "So you lost."

"I'm not a dog for him to command! Neither are you. So, yes. I lost. Because I don't jump when he points, and if I lost, then there was no argument. Nobody wants me to promote anything now. Maybe he'll leave us both the hell alone."

Terrence looked pained. "Why didn't you talk to me?"

My voice caught as I choked on all the unsaid hurts between us. "And say what?"

"What if I could get him to agree to one more shot? None of that promo bullshit? I know there's a fight in Charlotte on May twentieth he still has an open spot on the card for—"

"No."

"No?"

It was an easy answer for me. Looking at my brother and how incredulous he was, I realized things were far worse than I'd known. Arlo Specter was a man who was so morally repugnant, I didn't see how anybody trusted him, let alone gave him money. And somehow my brother trusted the man. Or at least believed he owed him. It was nauseatingly wrong.

"Terrence, I told you. I don't like him or trust him and I won't make him money for him. Anyway, Kate's prom is May twentieth. I promised I'd be in town."

May as well have waved a cape in front of a pissed-off bull.

"Oh. Okay. I see. I'm your brother but you know, you promised *Kate.*" Terrence slammed another locker with his hand. Another with his elbow. One more with his fist. My head could hardly take the noise.

"Terrence." I stood up. I needed to calm him down. Talk to him. Tell him what I knew so he'd understand where I was really coming from.

"No." He shoved his hand in my face. "Is she the real reason you fucked up the second you finally hit the big time? God forbid she let you off your leash, right? I can't look at you right now. We'll talk about this when I don't hate your face."

That knocked me back. "We have the same face."

"Not after that fight, we don't."

"Nice. That's real nice."

With a final slam, he left the locker room. I let him go, too stunned to say anything else.

I'd regret that decision forever. It was the last time we really talked. Two weeks later he was dead, and I'd go on to spend day… months…years, replaying that conversation, wishing I'd said a hundred things differently.

#

Kate

After a fitful night back at that bed and breakfast, I return to Alonzo's in the morning to meet with his roommate's band so we can get to know each other more and start practicing. Today there is someone else here, a girl named Cassie who has helped write songs that she's agreed to let us use.

I like most of the people here, and most importantly, I like the band's music. More than I thought I would. In fact, I'm afraid of how much. I told Ty I'd probably stick around,stay a while but I wasn't entirely sure. The last few years for me, I've been in one serious rut.

I came to Evergreen Grove mostly because Alonzo asked. Also because I've been so, so tired of feeling stuck. When Alonzo and Ty showed up, my only plans were the same ones I'd had for months. Jumping seemed way better than standing still.

If this doesn't work out, I'm not really sure what would be next.

Cassie is demoing a song she wrote, and I think this is the first time I've been excited since Ty told me he would take me to the prom. Of course, that never happened. I find myself alternately hoping that this experience will end better, and telling myself not to get too invested. I tell myself this even as Cassie's song washes over me, bursting bright on my tongue like drops of lemonade.

The song is vibrant and emotional, reminding me of Echosmith and sunshine. I love music for its ability to tell a story when I struggle to convey my own thoughts, and for its ability to share emotion, or to help a person get lost when they need to get lost, but rarely does a song get me as caught up as this one does.

She's singing about young love and grass fields and even though my own love life is one big mess, I can clearly envision the intent of the song in the lyrics.

"Perfect," I find myself saying aloud when she finishes her run through. "Honestly. It's great. But… Layla was saying you sing yourself? Don't you want to use this song?"

She smiles broadly. Cassie has such a girl-next-door look I would be wary of her if she weren't so nice. "I've got songs coming out of my ears, honestly," she says with a blush rising to her face. "Really. It's pretty much all I do in my spare time. Start sketching something out on a napkin and then I work it and rework it until eventually I never want to hear it again. The ones I don't get tired of, I keep. This one, it doesn't really fit me but I hated to just throw it away, you know?"

"No. Yeah. I mean, I'm glad you didn't. It's…" Like the lemon squares my dad used to make. "Amazing."

"Thank you. Your turn to run it through?"

"Let's do it." I grab the lyric sheet and take my place at the mic, tapping the page in front of me. I've read it over maybe a dozen times, but sadly I have to read something and repeat it dozens of times (plural) before it really sticks in my head these days.

I wait for the drummer to count me in. We start shaky. Then stop and start and stop again, making tweaks to the pace, the key, and the phrasing before finally we feel good about the song we've got.

Layla, along with her roommate, nods to me and tweaks a peg on her bass. "That was good. Let's run through it again."

So we do.

I want to run into the sun
The way we did when we were young
I want to find that place
For just the two of us

I lose track of what I'm singing when I look up and notice Tyler standing in the doorway between the garage and the house. He's obscured in shadow next to a kayak hanging on the wall, but my body always senses when he's nearby.

We get to the end of the song with me on autopilot, and launch into it again before moving on to some of the band's favorite covers of Coldplay, Adele, and Andra Day.

I'm a little shaky at the end. Whenever I've been singing for a long time, I always am. There's something about putting all of myself into a song, all of my energy, all of my intention and emotion, that leaves me tired and wrung out afterwards. Even if I had just woken up, I usually feel like I need another few hours of sleep after singing. I figure this is probably another side effect of the head injury, except nobody's ever been able to tell me for certain.

When we're done, I gather my things, greedily guzzling a bottle of water and accepting comments from a couple of the band members as well as other people who stopped by to listen. Alonzo, Cassie, some random people who live nearby.

"That was great," Cassie says to me again. "Listen, I sing on the weekends at Joe's Bar. If you ever want to stop in and join me on the microphone, give me a call. I bet I could get Joe to set up something for the whole band, too."

Wow.

Then I look up, and there's Ty again. Still. Staring. And closer.

He'd seemed still and distant after the kissing "incident" so I'd been figuring he'd want to stay clear. It surprised me to see him here listening at all, much less sticking around after. I grab the jacket I bought myself at the local college bookstore when I got into town and head for the mouth of Alonzo's open garage, chilly now that I'm no longer performing.

More so, feeling vulnerable that Ty of all people has seen me stripped bare.

Oh, sure, he's seen me without clothes. That's different. Making music is an entirely different kind of revealing. It's emotional. And a hell of a lot more intimate if you're doing it in front of someone you care about. In front of someone you've cared about since you were a nerdy fifteen-year-old.

"Didn't know you had the pipes to pull off such a moving rendition of 'Rise Up' like that."

I freeze, feeling his words warm my back even though we're not touching. My fingers curl slowly into a fist, inexplicably frustrated. "There's probably a lot you still don't know about me, Ty."

"There's a lot I do know. Saw you almost every day for three years."

"People change." Some of old Kate is still in me I think, but I feel so distanced from her.

"I'm sure you're right. You're definitely different from the Kate I knew in school."

"Yeah. I'm different. I changed when I got into that accident. Apparently concussions can do that. Sometimes when I remember who I was, it's like it's all just pictures. I can't tell if my memories are really mine or someone else's."

He shakes his head and kicks a rock in the driveway. "So you don't remember anything about how you felt about me?"

"I remember everything when it comes to you, Ty." I just don't know how to bridge the gap between what I feel now and what I remember then. I know the girl I was loved Ty. Head over heels, attached at the hip, donate a kidney kind of love. Do anything love.

The girl I am now sees him as both a friend and a comfort *and* source of pain. It's hard to know whether I want to run away or hold him close. Both, maybe?

See, this is the thing I like most about being able to sing. I can put myself in the skin of a person who has just fallen in love, or just broken up with someone painfully, or who's just been given the most precious gift on earth. I can feel those things so strongly when the words are coming out of my mouth in a way that I can't feel clearly myself anymore.

Inside my own head and heart, it's all a tangled wreck. I'm still fighting to see anything that makes sense.

I've wondered if that part of me broke when a truck smashed into us. It's not like I can ask the doctor, because if I ask if I'm I ever going to be able to love normally again, it's going to look like I'm insane. Or they're going to pat me on the head and think I'm being a stupid emotional female.

Still, I look at Ty and I know I loved him. Missed him when he was gone. One of my few clear memories after the accident is of him walking away from me in the ICU, after telling me I should never have been in that car.

I remember it hurting, but it doesn't hurt now. Mostly, I'm numb. Sometimes angry. When I stare at him though, I remember the spark that happened at the apartment. The flash of memory, of sensation, of *feeling.* I was in his arms and I felt like I belonged there, and it was the way things were supposed to be. Like they'd always been before.

So I kissed him.

It didn't make me suddenly feel normal again, but it kindled a warm glow in my belly that I can't erase. Like turning a burner on low and then leaving it that way. It's dangerous to leave the burner on, unused and unsupervised, but I can't locate the off switch.

He's staring with his hands in his pockets as if he expects I might say something else, and I don't know what else that might be, so I work on making myself scarce.

"Okay, well. I should go. I have…" To go and scream into a pillow. To take a long, long shower. "To go and lie down. As much as I love band practice, it's killer on my neck and shoulders."

"Hey." He steps around in front of me, sort of blocking my exit. Not really, because I could go around him, but certainly forcing me to face him first if I do. "You give any thought to what we talked about?"

"We talked about all kinds of things. Is this about muffins again?"

"The thing where you come with me to the gym and work out with me. I do think it would help."

"Yeah, maybe. I'm just not—not today, okay? I didn't sleep well. I'm tired."

He nods. "Okay. Let me walk you back, at least." Instead of waiting for me to answer, he simply steps alongside me and tugs my elbow with his finger, a sign that I'm expected to walk alongside him.

I know from experience if I don't comply, he'll grab my hand and pull me along, and today I'm a little too raw to handle that level of touchy-feely. So I go, even though I don't know why he's doing this.

"You don't have to walk me home. I'm sure you've got better things to do."

"It's no trouble. I have to meet Dante over at the gym later anyway. Your place isn't too out of the way."

"The gym is entirely in the other direction and this is practically Mayberry we're living in. I'm perfectly safe. Really, Ty. I can walk back on my own."

He grabs my hand, and even though it feels odd, I can never make myself pull away. Because it also feels oddly familiar, in a time when so often even my own body is unrecognizable to me.

"You can never assume anything," Ty murmurs. "And right now I'm gonna make sure you get home safe so you may as well let it go."

Now that… That affectionally pushy side to him I recall clearly. I remember liking it, before. I realize I also like it now.

12. NEGOTIATION

Ty

"I think you should reconsider about the gym. A good workout always helps me relax when I'm feeling achy and tired."

She drops her ridiculous Pender Tech spirit jacket on the neatly made bed when we get inside her room. Damn, I wish her new apartment was ready already. This place looks like a display room for antiques with all its clocks and knickknacks and the lacy bedspread and everything. Frankly, I don't know how in the hell anyone sleeps here. I'd be too afraid of getting that bedspread dirty.

"I appreciate what you're trying to do," she says, "but honestly all I want to do is take some painkillers and lie down."

I should let her go. She's old enough to make her own decisions and I don't belong here, telling her what's what. Can't, though. It doesn't sit right, the idea of just turning around and leaving her to fall apart. I made that mistake with Terrance, and it's left me empty to this day.

"How about a compromise?" With a gentle push, I hook my arm around Kate's shoulder to guide her over to the bed. "You got any ibuprofen around here?"

She stares me down before giving up a jerky and reluctant nod. "Um. Yeah." She points to the half-open door that reveals her en-suite bathroom. "In the medicine cabinet. Bottom shelf."

It's no easy feat to avoid looking around at the girl things in her bathroom. She's got underwear hanging from the edge of the tub and the shirt I loaned her over the towel bar. I could insist on getting it back, but I think I like having her in my clothes. “Got it.” I shake out three tablets and return the bottle. “Now I want you to try and find a comfortable position on that bed.”

She’s in a sports bra and jeans when I return. Staring from the other side of all that pristine lace, and suddenly I don’t mind so much the idea of getting that bed dirty. Not if I’m on it with her.

She’s too young, that old voice tells me.

She’s older now, insists that heady male hunger. The dark thing I feel inside me when I fight. When I’m so covered in fear and doubt it hurts to breathe. Those voices argue in my head now, while the pressure closes around my throat.

I close my eyes for a moment to get myself under control. “Seems like turning your neck is painful, so face up might be better.”

When I open my eyes again she’s already crawling across the bed. Torturing me by doing what I asked.

“Yeah. No way to lie on my stomach without turning my head to the side. So what are you planning to do?”

“Just wait.” I settle next to her with the anti-inflammatories and some water. “Take these first.”

Putting my hand on her back to help her sit brings the warmth of her half-clothed self and her smells—something flowery that’s probably from the toiletries the B&B provided—far too close for comfort.

She swallows them with a grimace and flops gently on the bed. “Thanks, but I’m telling you—”

“I’m going to make you a deal.” I pull off my Old Faithful sweatshirt—the one that’s been with me since high school and has been washed and worn so it’s the softest thing on the planet—and lay it over a mahogany rocking char.

"Deal?"

"No. Uh-uh. I see you tensing up like that. Stop." As carefully as I can, I sit myself at the end of the bed and pull atoff her shoes.

Her socks still have mud stains from the night we found her in that field. I rub at the tops of her feet and toss them on the floor.

"You need some new clothes, girl."

A smile slips across her face. "Says the guy who's been wearing the same Knicks sweatshirt since high school.

"Hey. My gran got me that shirt. You don't mess with gifts from a man's grandmother."

She smiles again. Almost lasts a solid two seconds. "I know. So what are you doing?"

With a bottle of fancy bed and breakfast lotion that I grabbed off the fancy bedside table, I'm warming a blob of something that smells like lavender in my hand and preparing to rub it on her feet. "Negotiation."

She lifts her head from the pillow and looks at me like I've lost my mind. "Excuse me?"

"Put your head down. Gonna strain your neck. Damn." I take one foot in both hands and proceed to massage the ball and her toes with the pads of my thumbs. "So my deal. From here on out, you're going to try the over-the-counter stuff first when you're in pain."

Her foot curls in my hand. Were I to feel any other part of her body, I'd surely find the rest of her tensing up. It all starts in the feet.

"Just try it first," I say again. With a press of my thumb, her foot yields under the pressure. "You put up a wall between a gentrified neighborhood and one that's got corner boys and squatters in abandoned buildings, it's not gonna make that struggling neighborhood go away. Wall only helps you ignore the problems while they get worse because they're being ignored. Got me? Same with your industrial-grade painkillers. Not fixing a damn thing, only covering up the problem."

A knot of tension gives way under my fingers. Her foot twitches in my hands and she blows out a breath of air. Her face is flushed, and her eyes have fallen closed, lips slack. As relaxed as she looks, I don't push her on an answer even though I want to. I know she heard me.

"Okay," she whispers at last. "I'll try."

When my fingers reach the back of bare heel, an quiet moan slips from her mouth. A male part of me responds. That sound, it's too primal.

"I can't believe I'm actually feeling more relaxed. How did you know this would work?" The wonder in her voice isn't doing anything to help calm me down.

"This massage therapist I was seeing, she taught me about how everything was connected. She had a special interest in reflexology, which is all about feet." Not that I wanted to lie, but I bet my answer throws some cold water on things.

For a minute I'm holding my breath. My thumbs are pressed to her ankle, her heel against my chest. She could do serious damage to me right now, and I wouldn't blame her if she did.

But she only smiles. "A foot fetishist, huh? Sounds like my kind of girl."

My stomach flops at the disappointing realization that she's not sounding in the least bit jealous at the same time my balls whip around as if to say, *Wait a minute, did she say she has a foot fetish? What other kind of fetishes does she have?*

I resume my foot rub and try to stay cool, but I'm fumbling and only half paying attention at this point. "Oh yeah? Since when did you get to be a girl with sexy fetishes?"

"Since always. Or never. It depends. You know how my mom tried to keep me sheltered, right? I guess since I wasn't allowed to *do* anything I spent a lot of time thinking about them. And looking them up on the Internet. And accidentally running across things I had no idea existed. Did you know there are entire websites devoted to people who like to have sex with their house pets?"

She makes a pretend horror face. I choke on my own tongue and drop her foot in my lap. I grab it again to avoid letting her feel what being here and touching her is doing to me.

And now she's laughing at me. I don't know whether to be glad or humiliated.

"God, Ty. The look on your face." She lifts her left foot. "Hey, there's a spot on this foot that pops all the time when I'm walking. Think you could massage that out for me, please?"

I raise my eyebrow. "Since you asked nicely. But only if you stop talking about animal sex."

She laughs again. Okay, hearing about that stuff was worth hearing her laugh. I try not to judge, but I have a definite hard limit when it comes to bestiality.

Suddenly she sobers up. "Hey, Ty?"

"Hmm." My head is down, focused on the spot she mentioned in her foot. I smile with satisfaction when it pops under my thumbs. "There it is," I murmur.

"You're just so tight all over, like I said. That didn't hurt, right?"

She shakes her head, looking dreamy and unfocused. "No, it feels good. Really good." She shifts down, pulling her foot out of my hand. "I haven't felt this good in a long time, actually."

I rub my hands together, and then over my arms and elbows, chasing chill bumps. I'm going to smell like lavender for a while, but at least I won't be ashy. "Well. Glad I could help. See, if you work on natural ways to relax and fewer prescription painkillers, I think you'll find you can get yourself back to feeling human a lot sooner. You've come a long way. Don't ruin it by falling slave to those pills."

"I'm feeling pretty human right now."

Her hand reaches towards mine. Any idiot in the world would know what that means, and I'm no fool. Question is, am I stupid enough to go back to a girl who once cut me from her life?

I shouldn't. Not when I know she's still it for me. Getting burned a second time is more than I'm willing to handle.

"Ty?"

Her eyes are heavy and tired when I turn her way.

"I remember being this girl with a crush. Always looking for you. Following you and watching you fight and waiting for you so you would hopefully walk me home after, but you never wanted anything more than to be a really chivalrous babysitter. Was it my age or was there something else? I wasn't good enough?"

"Hell no." It's the work of something I can't control when I lean forward to push my arms under her back and pull her against my chest. My lips are only a breath away from hers when I say, "Maybe I was afraid I couldn't handle your freaky sex fetishes."

She's laughing again. Damned if I couldn't get used to the feel of her breath on my cheek. Her body shaking against mine. "Well there's no way to know what I like for sure until I've actually tried it, you know?"

This girl's gonna kill me. I know it for sure. My hand tightens against her back. "That's pure evil. And so you know, it was never about you being good enough. It was about waiting for the right time. And not wanting to get my ass handed to me for screwing around while you were still in high school."

She glances down. "I'm not in high school any more."

"I know."

"Well." She reaches down. Gentle fingers practically tickle my side. "My schedule is open. Is now a good time?"

I don't move right away. I can't kiss her again without letting this thing reach its logical conclusion. Unless I keep on kissing her until we're both breathing hard and slick with sweat, and then I'll be the one left heartbroken.

If I couldn't keep this girl while she was half dead in the hospital, how do I keep her now? I'm just holding on to what little sanity I have.

She pulls back some. "Oh. I get it. You *do* still blame me."

"For the accident? I never blamed you."

I do still wonder what she was doing in that car. She and I were supposed to meet that afternoon and instead she was in the passenger seat next to Terrence, headed out of town. She's said she didn't remember the accident itself or what happened before. The guy driving the car sure won't spill. It doesn't matter anymore, I guess.

There's doubt all over her face. Hurt and worry that tightens my gut. A pout to her lips that makes her even more beautiful.

I love this girl. I have for years.

Will backing away from her save me any pain after all we've been through? Or maybe, just once, I could give up on fighting what I want and have the one thing I always grieved over missing, other than my family.

We'd talked about getting a hotel room on prom night. Prom night never happened. Maybe today we can get back one of the things we lost.

I gather her hair into my hands. Pieces of scar tissue meet my fingertips as I tunnel through soft strands and run my fingers over her scalp. The sound she makes sends a shiver down my spine.

I let the old hurt in my heart fall away as I put my hand to her cheek. For a second, her my breath stops when our lips brush.

#

Kate

Ty's kiss shakes something loose inside of me. Unlike before at the rental place, when we were there and close and just sort of leaned into each other like it was the natural thing to do, this is a statement. Whatever he's saying but I hear it loud and clear.

Inexplicably, tears sting my eyes. None of today was what I expected of him. I thought coming here to Evergreen Grove would hurt because of Ty, but over and over he's been the one easing my way. It's confusing and hard to think about, especially now when each breath gives me more of him. His smell, which is a subtle soap and rain combination that makes me remember the time he walked me home during a thunderstorm, and his touch, which is…

God, it's amazing. His hands are huge and confident and *everywhere.* I never imagined a man could be so reverent and so damn handsy all at once. He walks the line so well I want to laugh, except I'm afraid he'll stop if I do. Right now he's stroking the curve of my waist, and I have high hopes that hand will creep up under my sports bra and ease the tingling ache that I'm feeling just beyond the tip of his index finger.

"This feels good," I whisper against his mouth. Then, emboldened by desire, I grasp his hand and nudge it up under the edge of my bra, smiling when he groans against me.

It does feel good. *He* feels good, and it's amazing. I've spent God knows how much time and even more money trying to get outside of my body. With music if I could, with pills or alcohol or other dangerous behavior if I couldn't.

Feeling anything at all was an all-around negative. Feeling pleasure? Well, that simply wasn't on the table.

Sure, I've been interested in sex. The desire is there, and the parade of AA batteries that have gone through my vibrator would make you weep. Aside from a little fooling around at parties though, I've never wanted to go through the relative gymnastics of actually getting into bed with another person.

What if I tweaked my back? Pinched a nerve? I'm already pretty broken. What little good I had in my life disappeared along with my ability to enjoy day-to-day existence. What if I try to have sex and it's equally awful? A gal doesn't want to have everything outright ruined for her, you know?

But this is Ty. I may be jumbled up emotionally and my memory may be spotty, but I have remember him from before. The girl I used to be loved him. She trusted him enough to follow him anywhere.

Deep down, my body still knows him. Responds to him. I can't even pretend to ignore this. Not when so little good has come my way and not when he can erase the pain.

"This hurt? You okay?" He's pulled off his shirt and leaned forward, draping his upper body over mine.

I shake my head. Amazingly, no, it doesn't hurt. I thought the weight of a large body, especially one as large as his, would be too much to handle. "It feels like you were meant to be here."

"Maybe you're just stronger than you think." For a second his smile almost looks sad, but before I can figure it out, it's gone.

"Or you've got magic hands. My feet are permanently spoiled after that little massage thing you did."

He's both gentle and firm in his touch. The way his hand cups my shoulder and slides up my neck. "Then I guess I'll have to do it again sometime."

"Hey, Ty?"

He sits up. "Everything okay?"

"Yeah. I was just thinking if we're going to take this any further, we should both take off our pants."

His smile is big and wide, but his eyebrows dip together in uncertainty. "You sure that's what you want?"

My body is humming. Pulling toward him like he's the only thing it's ever wanted. "I'm completely sure."

Saying so sets my heart off at a brisk pace, both excitement and fear. The nervousness and the want braiding together in my bloodstream to create a long-burning fuse.

When he stands to push down his pants and underwear, I am not prepared. Oh, I know. I'm the one who said let's lose the pants, but Oh. My. Goooooood.

"So. I bet you work out."

He presses his fist against his lips, trying not to laugh. "I do what I can."

"Want to get over here and show me what else you can do?"

He slides along beside me, kissing my rib cage and my navel. I'm still wearing exactly what I started with, minus the jacket and shirt I removed myself when I entered the room.

"Hey, Ty? Is there…something you don't like about my body?"

He gives me a sharp look. "Why in the hell would you ask me a question like that?"

"Uh, because I'm insecure and you seem to be dragging out the part where you get me naked?"

Uh-oh. Now he's looking at me *patiently.* "You mean because you said you haven't had sex and I wanted to ease into things? Let you be in charge of taking off your own clothes?"

Oh. Okay. He's really good and I should've known better. "Yeah, about that." I reach up and pull off my sports bra, flinging it over the edge of the bed. "Can we, you know, not? With the foreplay. I'm nervous. Dragging this out will only make me more nervous. I'm good. Honestly."

He exhales a heavy, hot breath and shakes his head. "You know, so much about you is different. It's nice to know some of the old you is still in there."

"What the hell is that supposed to mean?" Great. Was that condescending? I think he sounded condescending. "This is going entirely the wrong way for getting me in the mood. Are you sure you actually want to have sex?"

He breathes a low chuckle against my belly button. I want to be annoyed that he's laughing at me but the sensation makes me shiver. He pops the button of my jeans and eases the zipper down slowly.

"Kate, there will be foreplay. And you're damn well going to like it."

He eases my jeans over my hips, followed by my exceedingly boring underwear. "Okay, pretend you didn't see those. I got them in the miscellaneous aisle at the grocery store."

"You wanna wear none at all, that's okay with me."

"Guys," I mumble. "You're all the same."

"Oh, that's where I beg to differ," he says in a voice that slides over me like silk, right before he parts my legs and makes me gasp so sharply I'm sure I'll never breathe again.

"Holy shit."

"Mmmm."

His tongue is doing wicked things between my legs. Wet, hot, incredible things.

I want to die. Right now. I want to die and have this be the last thing I feel. It'll be a good way to go.

"Ty, that's amazing."

He pushes my knee into a bent position and urges my legs wider, all of it so slow and gentle it's almost maddening. My hips move in small circles to try to capture the optimal pressure from his tongue, until the firm clasp of his hand holds me down.

A rush of tingles fan out from my core, spreading through my legs and up my back. Muscles that live in a perpetual state of tension ease as he works, all blissed out by the erotic attention from Ty's tongue.

All the time I've spent thinking about sex, and speculating on the good and the bad of it, I never imagined it feeling like this.

"Okay, Ty," I breathe. "You were right. Foreplay…foreplay is good."

He lifts his head, reaching for something out of frame of my periphery. "Good? That's all you got?"

What I've got is fucking amazing. I didn't know another person could make me feel like this. I'm shaking, and frankly a little frightened.

Frightened in a way that has nothing to do with losing my virginity to a big, musclebound fighter and everything to do with what it could mean to feel things for this guy again. Not the throat-clogging awe and affection I'm feeling. That wasn't part of the plan, and I'm not sure these emotions are something I can handle right now.

Seems a little late to worry about it though, doesn't it? So when he pulls a condom from his wallet and climbs onto the bed, I pull him down to kiss me before he can notice that I'm shaking.

13. AN AWKWARD PLACE

Ty

"You cold?"

She shakes her head but I can tell she's shivering. Or she's nervous. Maybe that's only me.

I've been with my share of girls. Since meeting Kate, every one of them has been a poor attempt at erasing her from my memory. This, being with her, it's what I've waited for since the day I first saw her standing in the crowd to watch me fight.

Nothing's ever perfect, but I want this to be. I wanted to be her first. I wish I could be her only.

I'm kneeling on the bed when she smiles and grips my shoulder. "Come here, already," she says.

"Oh, I'm coming."

Damn, this is like four times now I've gotten her to laugh? Not an all-out, belly-grabbing laugh, but still a decent chuckle. Compared to the way things have been, it's a huge improvement.

No longer afraid to kiss her, I claim her mouth the way I want. I taste the plump sweetness of her lips and ease my way inside with my tongue. I'm gentle, but I tell her in no uncertain terms that her mouth is mine. For that moment anyway, every piece of skin I put my hands on belongs to me.

"Ty…"

I bury my nose behind her ear, drawing in her smell. "Yeah, baby?"

"I've waited so long for you."

Those words are like gasoline in my blood and she just lit the match. "You think now's the time?"

Truthfully it's going to be a feat of great human will to hold back from not losing my mind here. This moment has to be right and good and special. My heart and my brain know better. My dick is arguing for other courses of action.

Her lips caress my ear. "Yeah. Now. Please, Ty."

With all the effort I can manage, I rock into her slowly. Even easing the way with my fingers and my tongue, I still worry about hurting her. Not only in the usual ways when you're with a girl who's a virgin, but she's still got pain from a serious car accident. One I want to think about as much as I want my dead grandma to walk in on this moment, but one I have to think of nevertheless because I'm bigger than Kate and if I'm too rough I could hurt her.

I use my elbows to hold myself up and press forward slowly, freezing when she sucks in a gasp of air. "What's wrong?"

"Nothing." Her chest rises and falls sharply, making me doubt her answer.

"You sure?" I'm deep inside her now, one head encased in tight heat and my other head freaking out because maybe I did something wrong. It's an awkward place to be.

"No. No. I—sorry. You pushed in and I tilted my hips and I don't know what it was but for a second it all felt…really good. Extra good. Sorry. I didn't mean to worry you."

"Nah. We're cool. All good." We're great. We're excellent. Now if I could just figure out what thing I just did and do that some more.

So I press in again, watching her face. Studying the swirl of light in her eyes from the window and the bedside table, and the way her lips part each time I push inside. So long as she looks like she's feeling good, then I'm good, too.

"Can I wrap my legs around you?"

"You sure you feel up to that?"

A gleam enters her eyes. "I know I'm injured, Ty, but I can still bend my legs."

"Then by all means."

Having her wrapped around me makes me go faster, harder, still watching her for signs of trouble but none come. Her eyes stay on mine, part wonder. Part challenge.

All I can do is touch her, letting my hands wander her neck and her chest, as if the feel of her skin will help solidify that she's really here with me.

She frowns when I slow my pace. "What's wrong? It's the scars, right? They're turning you off?"

It's only then that I realize I've been running my hand over a puckered line of skin above her left breast. "Baby, nothing's turning me off. I slowed down because I was so worked up that if I didn't back down, things were going to get embarrassing."

"Oh." She lets out a thin, nervous laugh. "God. I thought maybe…" She brings a hand to her chest, inadequate to cover what she sees as imperfections. Also unnecessary.

"Hey, hey." I take her hand in mine and kiss her. "You were always beautiful to me, and it had nothing to do with your body."

I guess that was the exact wrong thing to say. A tear slips down the side of her face.

"But I'm not the same anymore."

I surge forward, kissing her harder this time. My hand covers her chest, hiding the scars she finds so offensive. "You're still the same in here."

With a great big breath, she pulls my mouth to hers. I'm all too happy to keep right on making love with my mouth as well as my body.

Somewhere in the downstairs of the B&B, someone's turned on music. Some kind of jazzy riff, that's nothing I've heard before, or at least nothing I can hear well enough to identify. But there's a steady high-hat and an emotion-filled piano that pushes us both a little faster. A little harder.

"God. Yes," Kate breathes. She's closed her eyes, head back on the pillow. "That's so good. It's icy and white, like diamonds and snow."

What in the *hell* is she talking about? "Kate, are you okay?"

"Oh. God. Yeah. Nothing. That—that feels good. You feel good. Can I be on top?"

I have the weird feeling she's distracting me, but I'm too turned on to care. Seeing her on top of me? I want that. I want her body stretched out above mine.

I roll us carefully and let her get situated. "Oh, yeah. This is good. This is working for me." The sight of my hands on her hips. Her breasts swaying above me. I am more than okay with the entire thing.

At first she seems awkward with the position, but works out the rhythm pretty fast. For a moment, all I can do is lie there and watch. Her eyes are closed, her palms are braced on my chest, and her lips are open only the tiniest bit, with her hair sweaty and plastered to her face.

I could stare at her forever this way.

This is what I've missed out on, this past couple of years. I don't want to give it up for a minute longer. I'm not going to.

"Ty. This is amazing. I didn't think anything could feel this good."

Her release is almost a spiritual thing, with a sudden burst of afternoon light from the window and her eyes flying open as she gasps out her pleasure. She moves on top of me in undulating waves until I lose my control and dig my fingers into her hips, thrusting upward like it's the end of my life.

Maybe it is.

As I look at her there above me, I'm pretty sure I'm over. Done.

Hadn't I fed myself some line earlier about how it wouldn't make much difference if we got naked together because I already had feelings? Had I tried to tell myself I owned her body? Well, if this had happened in the octagon, I just lost by submission. And I can't own this girl, because I already gave her my soul.

How could I have forgotten? I lost that fight a long time ago.

#

Ty

Before our gran passed, Terrence and I had what I think a lot of twins have. Not that we went around in matching clothes or anything ridiculous, but he *was* my best friend. Fast forward to duking it out in a group home where I could tell he was keeping secrets from me, and then the foster family who took me "only wanted the happy one." Everything went to hell.

We tried to stay connected, but half the time we didn't even know where the other was. Our extracurriculars and after-school activities became lifesavers because they gave us ways to track each other down and hang out. Talk about our dreams of being champions. "Someday," we'd say. "You'll see," we'd say. Until we didn't.

I still wonder if that's what made him do what he did. Set up that title fight, push for it, even after all the times I said no.

I hate thinking he felt like that was the way to fix things between us. And that things got so ugly he died with that rift between us. I also hate that he's the one who left first.

Kate's arm tightens around my waist. "Are you okay?"

Because I don't want to put tension between us by bringing up Terrence, I say, "Yeah. Just thinking about food."

She lifts up like she's getting out of bed. "You're hungry? I don't have anything here except potato chips, but the lady who works downstairs will usually make me something for dinner if I ask nicely."

My hand tightening on her hip helps persuade her back down under the covers. "Now, we don't need to get fancy."

"Well, there's not a lot to eat in this town. There's that coffee shop-slash-bakery place you took me to, but they close in the afternoon. There's that fancy place in town, which is even more expensive than here, plus I'd have to walk there. I won't have a kitchen until my new apartment is ready, and I don't usually feel up to a bumpy bus ride to anywhere farther."

She rolls onto her back. There's a piece of her hair wrapped around her finger, making me wonder if she's nervous. And what I can do to relax her again.

"Wasn't trying to judge. We can eat wherever you want."

My idea of fancy is a restaurant that doesn't give you your food on disposable dishes. I can adapt. Especially if it shuts down the tension crackling around her all of a sudden.

I slide over next to her and press my front to her side, taking hold of that nervous hand and rubbing her palm with my thumb. "What's going on here, huh? You used to twist your hair around your finger when you were anxious."

Her cheeks turn a pretty shade of pink that matches the roses in her pillow shams. "My mom kept mentioning that to me. I don't really remember, but I guess nervous habits are one of those things you do without thinking. It's probably super obvious now because my hair is so short, and I'm sure I do it even more now because—*god*—I'm just this huge ball of stress ever since—" She squeezes her eyes shut tight. "Sorry."

Yeah. "We have to be able to talk about what happened."

"I know." But even though her words agree with me, her body's turning away and pulling the sheet up to cover the skin she'd let me run my hands and eyes all over minutes ago.

"Hey." I reach around to cup her chin. She's got those issues with her neck and I don't want to hurt her, but I do need her to look at me. "Kate. Hey."

I don't usually put so much force in my voice with her. But it works. To my surprise, her eyes open and she turns.

"Don't you think it's time we found a way forward?"

There's a hard, steady pound in the center of my chest. A painful phantom feeling in that place where my heart used to be. It feels an awful lot like a warning.

It feels like an eternity I've loved this girl, but she took herself away from me once already. I've lost my twin, the half of myself I thought would be in my life forever. It aches every day, being without Terrence, and coming to Evergreen Grove to be close to the one friend who knew him well hasn't turned out so great. Alonzo clams up when I try to talk about Terrence, too.

I miss Terrence like a limb that got cut off but still throbs. And if the girl I love, the girl who sat next to him in the car the day he was killed, won't talk to me about him either? I don't know what else I have.

"Maybe you're right," I say when the silence stretches too thin. "Maybe this was all a mistake."

"I just don't want you to blame me." She hugs her arms to her chest and turns, eyeing me as if she's never seen me before. Funny, since I'm naked in her bed.

"You've said that before. Why would I blame you?"

"Because you did. In the hospital. My memory is spotty, but I know you came. I heard you say I shouldn't have been in the car and it was all my fault."

"No. No. Okay, first? That's not what I meant. I blamed *myself* for you being in that car. And second, they told me you were sedated with pain meds, and if I'd known you could hear me I would've been more careful with my words. Is that why you didn't want me come back to see you?"

"What do mean?"

My mouth about hits the mattress. "One of my foster moms had been a nurse, which was how I got in to see you the first time. I tried to visit again the next day and your mother was there. She said you didn't want me there. It wasn't good for your recovery."

She lets out a long sigh. "Ty, you know how my mom is. She probably hoped if you stopped coming around, I'd succumb to her wishes and meet a nice boy from her crazy church. She didn't even want me *in* the hospital at all. I think if my dad hadn't still been living there when the accident happened, I'd be dead by now. He was the one who consented to treatment."

I squeeze my hand in hers. "You really think your mom would have tried to faith heal you after a damn car wreck?"

The idea boils my blood. Here this girl is, still struggling to get herself together more than a year after that wreck. She'd had a head injury and broken bones, for crying out loud. My gran always prayed when people were hurt, but it didn't stop her from going to the doctor.

"Ty, this isn't like your grandmother's church, with all the singing and praising and hugging and potato salad after. When I broke my arm riding my bike when I was eleven, she wanted to pray over it to make it better. I had to beg to go to the hospital because it hurt so much I couldn't change my clothes. I've heard of kids in her church dying from treatable illness and the parents and church elders lamenting that it must have been God's will. So maybe, if they'd refused treatment and I'd died from my injuries, that would've simply been God's will too."

That suggestion freezes me on the inside. Makes me need to touch her more, pull her close. The idea that I could have lost her and Terrence both that day, over her mother simply saying no to medical care is something I can't handle.

"Thank goodness your father intervened."

She shakes her head. "Well, the paramedics and ER doctors had started on me before my parents showed up, and once I had a say, I wasn't going to do it her way. My mom and I have fought about it ever since. She's on the naughty list with her precious church and it's my fault. She's also on the naughty list with me because I kind of thought I should be more important than what her fellow hat-ladies think."

"You should have been." My lips press to her shoulder. "You are to me. Which is why I need you to start taking better care of yourself, okay? After everything you've come through, you deserve better than to wind up broke and hooked on pills."

She squeezes my hand. "I'm going to try, Tyler. I promise."

That thumping in my chest is growing stronger. Steadier. If I didn't know better, I'd almost think that was a real heart beating in there. Maybe I'm alive after all. Maybe thanks to Kate. Maybe I needed her to be here, so I could live, too.

14. OUT OF FOCUS

Kate

We wind up making love again. As much as I hate that phrase, that's strangely the way it feels. Ty's presence, everything from the sound of his voice to the intensity of his eyes, brings me back to a someone I'd forgotten I could be. A someone who doesn't hurt.

So when he hovered above me so carefully and brought that pouty lower lip to brush mine, I couldn't keep from sliding beneath him and opening up. I shivered at the way he already felt so right inside me, and pretended I only needed him to pull the blankets over our bodies.

No, I'm not confused by my feelings. Not at all.

Somehow I expected something different from this experience. Mutual pleasure, certainly. Finally ridding myself of the great invisible V on my forehead, also a bonus. Remembering Ty to be someone the old me had trusted, double bonus.

I did not expect those feelings to rekindle. Or to…whatever it is they're doing. Am I remembering something I used to feel or am I feeling new things all over again? Honestly, I don't know. I do know that standing under the spray of a hot shower with the most phenomenal set of hands in the world massaging my back is doing strange and scary things to my brain.

"This okay?"

I put my hand over his arm. "Sure. Why?"

"You seem distracted."

"Just thinking about how great this showerhead is, you know? Perfect temperature, perfect pressure. I could stay in here all day."

With him. In this nice little bubble where the only thing we have to worry about is finding something to eat and being together. Outside there will be other things. Issues. Questions will come up or people will decide we don't belong together.

Right now is the best I've felt since I woke up in that hospital full of tubes and morphine.

He kisses my shoulder. "This right here is pretty perfect, if you ask me."

Amazingly, I feel my lips curl into what feels like a smile. A real one. "You're sweet."

"So are you," he whispers in my ear. "Remember, I had my mouth between your legs, earlier."

My ankle wobbles for only a second, but he notices. A strong arm tightens, gentle but firm around my waist. A rush of warmth I can't describe floods my body. "So…you want to get something to eat after this?"

"Hmmm. Much as I'd like to, I probably ought to go by the gym. Dante thinks I've got a shot at jump-starting my career again, and he also had some dealings with the guy who…you know…took advantage of Terrence."

Suddenly I don't feel so warm, in spite of the shower beating down. "Like what kind of dealings?"

He shakes his head. "We're still feeling each other out. Trying to see if we trust each other. I don't have a lot of information yet."

My brain throbs forcefully and so abruptly that I could swear I just got in a head-on collision all over again. Except I'm still here in the shower, with the magic fingers of water pressure beating gently on my shoulders. "I don't under— Oh. God."

You have no idea what I've done to make things happen for him.

Terrence's face bursts into my memory. So much like Ty's but at the same time so different, with its perpetual scowl and his right nostril flared slightly in a subtle sneer that he seemed to save especially for me.

I can remember him saying those words, but the moment is blurry and out of focus.

Things get floaty. I see myself talking to Terrence. Arguing with him while the world spins around us, super fast the way things spin when you've had too much to drink. I can't get him to listen and when I reach for him, I put my hand through smoke.

"Kate. Kate!"

I blink, only to find myself on the floor of the bathroom with Ty, a towel around my shoulders and a pair of worried brown eyes staring me down.

"What happened?"

His face creases into a frown. "I was going to ask you the same question. We were talking, and then you sort of slumped against me. I thought I was going to have to find you a doctor. Pretty much the only thing I don't know how to get to around here."

God, how embarrassing. "I'm fine. I don't need a doctor. I do think maybe I should lie down, though."

My equilibrium is returning but a strange nausea and lightheadedness lingers.

He shakes his head. "Probably all those meds you take. Bet this stuff will pass once you cut down."

Yeah, that's what it was.

I do my best to smile. "You're probably right."

"Come on. I'll get you into bed and see if that nice lady downstairs can get you something to eat."

"I don't think I'm hungry now."

"You'll need something later. Just in case, for when you're feeling better. Try it for me, okay?"

"Okay. Thanks, Ty. You're a good guy."

He gives me a handsome grin. "My gran would be proud." His eyes light up when he grins that way, looking warm and comforting and all too easy to fall into. If I'm not careful, I could fall for this guy.

Fall for him again. More. *Harder.*

Old me would be one hundred percent on board with that plan. New me has promised not to need anyone that way anymore. It's too easy to be hurt, and I'm already in pain every day.

People who are supposed to love you most can also break you into the tiniest pieces. I'm already awfully broken. I can't handle being broken by him, too.

#

Ty

Text from Tyler to Dante: *Hey. Sorry about yesterday. An emergency came up. I can swing by this morning sometime if you're around??*

Text from Dante to Tyler: *Sure. My fiancée is already working on her end-of-year project for school. Right now I pretty much live here.*

Text from Kate to Tyler: *Thanks for staying last night. Sorry about the part where I sobbed on your chest like a small child. Sometimes my brain goes a little haywire.*

Text from Tyler to Kate: *Hey. It's all good. Glad I was there for you. Take it easy today, okay??*

Text from Kate to Tyler: *Well I've got no band practice and you're busy, so I guess that's what I'll do.*

Text from Tyler to Kate: *B good and I'll bring you some dinner later. Something "fancy"*
Text from Kate to Tyler: *You're sweet. I hope it's baked oatmeal.*
Text from Tyler to Kate: ¯\(°_o)/¯
Text from Dante to Tyler: *Hey, punk. I've decided as your penance, you can stop by Delia's and get me coffee. Cassie knows my usual.*

Evergreen Grove is quiet at six in the morning. Back home you'd have garbage trucks and buses rumbling past and people getting started with their struggle to make ends meet. Here, I pass the occasional car and one friendly jogger, but mostly it's just me walking alone.

I take my time along the tree-lined roads (mostly Evergreen, which explains the town name I guess) instead of running this morning. Gives me a chance to take in the homes—most of them moderate in size but comfortable, some with smoke coming from storybook chimneys—all nicely kept and attractive.

The neighborhood where Kate's staying, those houses are big and way over-the-top for my taste. I'd like to think even if I had the money for that sort of thing, I wouldn't go buying a place with so many rooms you had to come up with stuff to do in them. The ones closer to Main Street though, seeing them causes an eerie sensation in my center. I'd almost call it longing, except I don't waste my time on feelings like that.

I guess maybe I get why Alonzo kept that house the lady who adopted him left. He's always saying he hates the place, but I can see how it would be nice to have something that's all yours. Growing up with a twin, nothing was ever mine. Even if it was mine, it was his, too. Not that I would've exchanged that to be without him.

When I turn onto Main Street I'm suddenly tired, which doesn't bode well for the rest of my day. I tell myself it's because I was up half the night worrying about that strange fainting episode Kate had and not because of my brother or what he thought of her is on my mind.

That girl's a distraction. Mark my words.

I feel like his ghost is following me as I walk in the door to Delia's Bakery and Café. It knows where I was yesterday, and it's judging me.

"Leave me alone," I mutter under my breath.

Only to look up and find myself face-to-face with one perky-as-hell sorority girl.

"Good morning." Girl smiles so bright I almost feel the need to shield my eyes. "You must be Tyler."

"I…am." I look around, but nobody's in the sparsely filled café that I recognize. One table has an old dude chomping down on a muffin, and behind the counter is a surly looking white dude with colorful tattoos who's either a possessive boyfriend or the heavy security for the coffee shop.

Sorority Girl shrugs and gives me a "What can you do?" smile. "Small towns. You know."

"I'm beginning to. You must be Cassie."

She holds out her hand. "I am. So nice to meet you. I think we crossed paths briefly at the Feral Monkeys band practice. Anyway, what can I get you?"

We shake hands and I take another glance at my phone to see if Dante's added anything to his order. He hasn't. "Uh, large coffee with skim milk and whatever Dante usually gets. He said you'd know."

She turns away with another bright, dimpled smile and gets to work. Across from me, muscle guy finishes his coffee and sets it on the counter. "Tyler. I'm Jake. You're going to be working for Dante?"

Damn. Small towns. Gossip really does travel faster than anything else. "Looks that way."

He bobs his head. "Great news." He leans over to give Cassie a quick kiss. "I'm outta here." He points to me. "Swing by Joe's Bar sometime and say hello. We're right upstairs." He turns his hand, pointing up at the ceiling above where we're standing.

He kisses Cassie again and with another, "Thanks for the coffee, babe," he's out the door.

"Okay, here you are." Cassie slides two cups across the counter. "Two large coffees, one with milk." With that, I get a giant exaggerated wink.

"What's with the wink?" And what's that smell? I smell chocolate from somewhere. All men have their weaknesses, and that rich hot cocoa smell is one of mine. Gran used to make it for us on chilly mornings.

She clears her throat. "Dante's favorite drink doesn't exactly scream health nut, and since he runs a gym, we like to help him save face. Not like it's a well-kept secret, but…"

Ah. "So what is it really?"

"Raspberry hot cocoa. Extra syrup."

Yeesh. Taking a whiff, it does smell amazing. "Whole milk in here?"

"It's creamier that way."

Wow. "Okay. Well. Thank you."

I reach for my wallet but she stops me with a hand. "On the house. Be sure to tease Dante mercilessly for me, and we'll call it even."

Small Towns: Even Weirder Once You Scratch the Surface.

Thanking her again, I head out and take my coffee and Dante's diabetes in a cup across the street to the gym, where I hand him his "coffee" with a big wink like the one Cassie gave me.

He takes the cup with a scowl. "Lemme guess. Cassie spilled my secret."

A young woman about my age is over in the corner with the jump rope. She laughs so hard she trips on the rope. "Dante, it's not a secret. Everybody knows. Literally everyone."

"You mind your own business, LeeAnne, or I'll make you run speed drills."

Her pale skin flushes from across the room and she returns to whatever she was working on.

"So. Next time you can't make it, do me a favor and let me know, all right? I don't mind if you have to bail. I mind if you do it without any kind of word. If I learn I can't trust you to respect my time, I'll wonder if I can trust you at all."

"That's fair." I don't trust easily, so I get that. If I want this situation to work out, I need to put in more effort.

I figure I should offer some kind of explanation. "I should explain that I'm not one to skip out on things, but my friend was sick and I didn't want to leave without making sure she was okay."

He nods and tosses me some protective gear. Somehow he's taken it on himself to be my trainer even though he's specifically said he doesn't do that sort of thing. "Let me guess. It's complicated?"

Well…it *is* complicated. "I'm making it as simple as I can."

He chuckles and shakes his head. "Good luck with that."

Across from me in the practice ring, he's assumed a fighting stance. He's waiting for me to acknowledge that we're starting, but I'm distracted by an old anger rising in my throat. Dante is a nice guy, a guy who says he has a DA interested in going after Arlo Specter if I can give good enough information, and it would be in my best interest to focus on being nice to him.

But the words shove into my throat and out my mouth like vomit before I can manage to take control. "What do you mean good luck? You gonna tell me I should dump her, too? She's a distraction? I'll never be a champion if I've got her weighing me down?"

Dante straightens up slowly, letting out a low whistle. "Hey, now. Is that what I said?"

"You didn't have to. I've heard it before."

He taps his gloves together. "Real talk? Plenty of fighters have girlfriends but it's no picnic. I didn't, but I knew guys that did. Some were serial cheaters. The ones who stayed faithful usually brought their significant others on the road with them. It's not even about all the groupies. You know the training involved. If you make it big, there's a ton of travel. These things put strain on a relationship. And if you do decide to sit down and tell me more about your brother so we can see if it might help the case, that's gonna be additional time and strain. Especially if you have to testify."

He pauses. Maybe he's expecting me to reply or maybe he's just letting it sink in. I do neither, letting the knowledge wash over me with a stubborn refusal to understand.

"I just think," he continues, "that right now you need to decide what it is you want most. And I'm not even trying to be a dick here. I've seen a lot of people drive themselves crazy with contradicting goals. You want to try and get justice for your brother? Give yourself that second shot? Date that girl you always had a crush on? You can't please everyone so be clear on what matters most."

I nod in understanding, but inside I'm covering my ears like a kid who doesn't want to be told no. I don't see why I can't do all of the above. I can spend time with Kate, I can come here to the gym to train when I'm not with her. I can teach my dinky one class a week, and I've only done a few local fights anyway. If I happen to get any that require me to leave town, that's a bridge I'll cross later.

It's all going to be fine. I've gone without for too long to let go of the things I want.

15. HANDSOME LIMESTONE ARCHITECTURE

Kate

Text from Tyler to Kate: *Looks like I get to meet my new students for the first time this evening. Ok if we have dinner tomorrow instead?*

Text from Kate to Tyler: *Sure but I'm keeping that T-shirt of yours as payment.*

Text from Tyler to Kate: *You mean you were planning to give it back?*

Text from Kate to Tyler: ... *No.*

Text from Tyler to Kate: (Middle finger emoji)

Text from Kate to Alonzo: *Hey. Looking for a PT clinic. Don't suppose you know of any?*

Text from Alonzo to Kate: *Is that a Pokemon thing? Try the comic book store on Poplar St. Or actually it's just a guy in his mom's basement with lots of disposable cash and free time, but his collection of action figures is impressive. So are his BJ skills.*

Text from Kate to Alonzo: *Thanks for the TMI.*

Text from Alonzo to Kate: *Yo. You texted me. I'm about ten seconds from a coma right no...ha. Had you going, I bet.*

Text from Kate to Alonzo: (Middle finger emoji)

I give up on Alonzo in frustration. After breakfast (Baked eggs with maple-bacon stuffing. Who knew? Oh. M. Gaaaahhd.), I manage to find Sierra, the sweet girl who checked me in when I got to town. Mealtime and hallway chats have revealed that her aunt owns the place but for health reasons or whatever, it's Sierra here most of the time. Frankly, being around her makes me question my life choices. She's barely any older than I am, and already running a bed and breakfast on her own?

What have I done lately? Mostly marathoned *Twilight*. Yes, I was in a serious car accident. Ty's right though. There's more I could be doing to take control of my health. My entire life. Now that I'm away from my mother and the strain of her ever-present judgment, it's time I do.

"Hey, Sierra. Great breakfast this morning."

"Thanks." She turns fire-engine red at the compliment. Seems to happen pretty much every time. Then again, I'm not so great at taking compliments myself. What is it about society that makes it bad for women to think good things about themselves?

"So listen, I was hoping you could help me."

"If I can, I'll be happy to." She stops in the middle of folding some table linens. It seems there's me and only one other couple staying at the inn, and the couple never comes to breakfast but she still sets all the tables in the morning so we can sit wherever we want. Feels like overkill, and this is why I'd suck at hospitality.

"So, Sierra. I was in a car wreck a year ago. Big one. Head and back trauma and everything. I'm sort of still getting back on my feet. I'm hoping to find a physical therapist or something in the area. Do you have any idea who I'd talk to?"

"Oh. Sure. There are a couple of people. Dante, over at the gym, I've heard is good with some injury-type stuff, and then if you go over to Pender, where the college campus is, student health has a sports-medicine department; I know there's physical therapy there. There has to be. It's an itty-bitty school but they still have athletes, and athletes get injured. If they can't help you over there, they can sure point you to whoever can."

"Perfect. Thank you. Can you tell me how to get there?" As much as Dante seems like a nice guy, I know Ty is over there and I'm not sure I'm ready to see him again outside of the room where we got naked together.

Right now I don't know how I'm supposed to act. We didn't talk about whether we're friends with benefits, or if that was just a one-night stand, or…?

It feels easier, albeit slightly cowardly, to skirt the issue. Besides, as much as I appreciate Ty's offer, going to an actual physical therapist seems like the better idea. I want to get stronger and healthier, and it feels like that includes *not* making him the guy I lean on for everything.

Using Sierra's directions, I take a local connector bus to the campus and make my way toward the building where she said student health would be located. It's a pretty campus. Quiet, probably due to the cold, but still populated with the occasional student hustling to class and a frosty landscape dotted with handsome white-stone architecture.

The building directory is tacked to a wall right above a couple of students who are making out with a great deal of enthusiasm. Their heads weave back and forth with just enough zag and zig that I can't get a handle on anything except that X-ray is on the second floor.

"Hey. Uh, guys? Guys. Yeah." Okay. They're ignoring me. I'm used to that. But when you're five-five and a buck ten, you learn how to get people to pay attention.

So I pick one, a strawberry-blonde with her hair in a ponytail, and tap her on the back with two fingers.

"Hi. Excuse me. So sorry to interrupt, but the directory seems to be right where your faces are stuck together, and I can't see through you."

Her companion, a sunny-looking young thing in a brown pixie cut, smiles up at me as if I didn't just interrupt their make-out sesh. "Ohey. I intern for Doctor Eaton. What department are you looking for?"

"Uh, PT?"

"Suite 307. Ask for Ollie, he has a much better grasp on physiology than the other guy."

"Oh. Great. Thanks. And, uh, sorry again for interrupting. As you were, and stuff."

I wave goodbye awkwardly and get on a bumpy elevator full of students. With a deep breath, I realize how tired I am and how sore my back is from the walk and bus ride. It's unlikely I'll even be able to get an appointment with anyone today, to boot. I didn't have a number though, and even if I had, it's easier for people to say no to you over the phone. So this was better, but the idea that I'm going to have to turn around and go back home without taking the precious prescription narcotics I've grown accustomed to leaning on is making me want to cry.

It feels like it's been hours when I finally locate a door unobtrusively labeled "Physical Therapy," with a cartoon picture of medieval torturers stretching a victim on the rack.

Someone's drawn an arrow toward one of the hooded figures with a name bubble that says "Ollie." The other says "Victor" with a pair of devil horns. Awesome.

An attractive guy with a swimmer's build and a man-bun approaches where I'm standing in the doorway. "May I help you?"

Please be Ollie. My back is on fire. I need something to go my way. "Please tell me you're Ollie. I was told to ask for Ollie."

He holds out a hand. "I am Ollie."

Ollie has one of those delicious accents that make women want to rub against a guy's leg and purr. I'm betting this college campus gives him plenty of play.

"Great." We shake. "So here's the thing, Ollie. I don't know if you can help me or not. I was in a car wreck a while ago and I've moved from the place where I was doing PT. I'm still in some pain and I'm trying to come up with a way to get myself back in shape. I'm hoping you might be able to help me, or point me toward someone who can."

"Do you have a PT prescription?"

Uh. No. "The original one ran out. I stopped going but I'm still having a hard time getting my strength back."

He looks uncomfortable. "Right. Are you a student here?"

Arg. "Not…exactly." Or at all. "Is there maybe a private clinic you'd recommend, if you can't help?"

He frowns at me. "St. John's Hospital is twenty minutes away. They have an Ortho and PT office. What kinds of problems are you having?"

"Uh…" After going from one doctor to another after the accident, I got used to cataloging my list of complaints. I haven't done it in a while, not for someone who knows the lingo better than I do, and it feels so strange I actually find myself laughing.

"So aside from overall muscle weakness and soreness, I've got hypermobile sacroiliac joints and a fused L-3 and L-4, both of which were caused or at least made worse by the accident. Also severe sciatica that makes it hard to sit for long periods of time, wrist pain, neck pain, and migraines."

He nods, stroking his chin. "I can usually tell how many doctors a person's been to by their grasp of buzzwords. You've been to a few doctors."

"I didn't even tell you about the work they did to my orbital bone."

"Points for orbital bone."

"Thanks." This guy seems cool. It sounds like he can't treat me if I'm not in school but he's being nice anyway, and I like him.

After a moment of what looks like intense thinking, he goes to a filing cabinet and pulls out a few papers. "Here. I can't treat you, but here are some exercises and stretches that target the areas you're complaining of trouble in. Someone with a solid grasp of their injuries like you have, you should know your body well enough to know if you're overdoing or an exercise isn't working. Do these three to five days a week for a month, see where your progress is. And if you get hurt and wind up in traction as a result of those exercises, we never even met."

I grab the papers from his hand. "Thank you."

I'm two steps toward the door when I hear, "Hey. I didn't get your name."

"Kate."

"You wanna get something to eat sometime, Kate?"

I pull my phone from my pocket. No new text messages from Ty. We made no plans for getting together today, no promises that we were suddenly dating.

Even so, I can't go agreeing to a food-grabbing thing with the handsome PT man. Even if I wanted to, which… I mean, he's cute, but he's not Ty. Not that I'm getting attached or anything. To Ty. I'm not.

Or I am. Fine. There.

"I'm flattered, but I'm sort of involved with someone."

He nods and a strand of hair falls from his stylish bun before he comes back to say one more thing. "Well listen, if you wind up back here as a student, I hope I'll see you in here again. You sound like you know your stuff. Could be a good line of work for you."

"Oh, no, I couldn't…"

Huh. I hadn't actually ever thought about doing something like PT. I was usually too busy feeling sorry for myself about how much pain I was in or feeling guilty for my hand in Terrence's death.

"Give it some thought." He presses a card into my hand. "If you come back as a student, look me up. And please. No pressure. Date-wise or otherwise."

"I will. Thanks."

I take my papers and his business card and leave, wandering the campus instead of going straight toward the bus stop. I find a seat in front of what announces itself to be the student center, and tap out a message to Ty: *Hey, what would you think about me enrolling in school?*

Tyler: *I'd think it sounds great. Just don't go throwing me over for any pretty college boys.*

Kate: *I've already gotten some flattering offers.*

Tyler: *I'm cuter. See?*

He sends me a picture of a kitten playing with string.

It's hard sometimes to infer meaning from text messages, but this time the meaning seems pretty clear. I smile and inhale the crisp winter air, feeling for once like I'm of value to someone else and liking it.

#

Ty

Tuesday afternoon my body aches when I make it back to Alonzo's place. I've been sparring with Dante and had an afternoon of teaching six kids under the age of twelve because Dante thought we should up the class to two days a week. Also, I was with Kate twice the night before.

I'm in desperate need of about sixteen solid hours of sleep. Some food. A shower. Not necessarily in that order.

What I'm hoping is that most of Alonzo's roomies will be at class or sleeping off their hangovers this time of day, so I can get a good long time to rinse off and then crash on my crappy cot in Alonzo's basement.

Alonzo would give me a better place to sleep if I asked, but I have my issues sometimes. The times when my thoughts get me in such a mood that the only person I can stand to be around is myself. Or lately, Kate.

I'm about to go up the stairs that will take me to the upstairs bathroom—the one with the good showerhead—when a voice breaks me out of my thoughts.

"Hey, there he is. Look what the cat horked up."

"*Alonzo.*" I slap a hand on the stair railing, amazed as ever at the thumping in my chest where I thought I'd gone numb. "The hell are you doing, man?"

He's splayed out across half of his sectional sofa with his hand in what I can only hope is a bag of Cheesy Cadoodles. If not then his hand is orange for a different reason and I don't even wanna know.

"Sorry, dude. Just watching wrestling. Haven't seen you around in a few days. You been hanging out with Kate?"

"So what if I was?" I hear accusation in his tone. "Isn't that what you wanted? You wanted me to go with you to bring her back here, and you didn't expect I was going to want to spend time with her again?"

"What I wanted was for us all to be a team again. Not struggling and scattered to the winds the way we have been. But think about it, Ty. Do you really think you and her hooking up is a good idea?"

This is too much. Really honestly too much. "Of all people, Alonzo, I expected you to be cool. Seemed like you were the one trying to push us together."

"Oh I'm cool. I'm as brisk as a polar bear swim, big guy. It's you I'm worried about. You've been mooning over this girl like a lost puppy since high school. She's not the same anymore and the two of you have immense pieces of baggage between you. Elephant-sized baggage. Crazy as that shit is, it's the exact same baggage but from different angles. You walked away from each other and didn't speak *one single word* to each other for a long damn time. I just don't want to lose you both if it all explodes again."

Not sure what pisses me off more, him calling me a lost puppy or the prickling sense deep inside my head that maybe Alonzo might have a point about something. We do have the same baggage, Kate and I. Terrence is my brother. She was with him when he died.

She asked me if I blame her. And I don't. But I do have unanswered questions.

Still though. I refuse to believe that it means we can't be together. And I refuse to look at Alonzo's smiling face, with his twitchy eye from getting high all morning and cheese residue on his fingers.

He's messed up right now and he doesn't know what he's saying.

"You wanted me to care about her again. Well, you win. I care. Now you're telling me I shouldn't care too much because we've both got baggage. All of this coming from a guy whose current life consists of smoking pot, mowing the town lawns for minimum wage, and a series of quickies in bathrooms. Where the fuck do you get off telling me how I should deal with my love life, man?"

"Hellooo. Ty threw out the F-bomb."

"Well you pissed me the fuck off." My grandmother would wash a grown man's mouth out for using that word in her house. To this day I don't say it unless I'm highly motivated.

Alonzo staggers to his feet, throwing the Cheesy Cadoodles bag in the general direction of the kitchen. "Hey. I'm trying to help you here."

"Yeah, well, like my gran said, it isn't helping if no one asked you for it."

"Oh, Jesus," Alonzo mutters, sweeping his mess of hair back from his forehead. "You and those fucking quotes from your dead grandmother. You got anything original to share with the class?"

"Holy— And just what the hell is your problem?"

"My problem is I finally got my friend back. Finally got both of you back, and you're going to fuck it up. All for a girl who—look, I love her and all—but she's pretty messed up in the head right now, so it's not like you can count on—"

When the redness of my anger clears, I've shoved Alonzo over the sofa and through the living room. All the way into the open kitchen, pinning him against the countertop bar that separates the two rooms. "Man, you know damn well I can kick your ass. You do not get to talk about her that way. You shut the fuck up right now."

Alonzo goes silent. His face shows me nothing but sadness and defeat.

"What in the hell is going on with you?"

Alonzo twists away and gives me his back, putting his hands down on the kitchen counter like he's bracing for impact. I could force him to face me but I don't. Whatever he's going through, it looks like he's struggling plenty as it is.

"Alonzo…Buddy…"

"I miss him, too, you know?"

"I know you do, man. We all do. I never said you don't get to miss him. Did I say something to make you think that?"

Alonzo shakes his head. "I just thought maybe having my best friends around again, it wouldn't feel so empty. But you're drifting, and Kate is hurting. This was my last-ditch effort to keep you both from floating out of my life. I'm going to lose you both anyway."

"You're afraid for *us*? Buddy. How many sex partners have I seen you parade through this place in the time I've been crashing here? How much drinking have I seen you do? How may times have I seen you high? You think you're the only one who's worried? What you're doing, it's no way to live."

My friend stares me down with tortured eyes. "So what's the way then? Smiling so hard nobody notices you're hemorrhaging? Your way?"

His words twist my stomach. Maybe because part of me knows that he's right.

We're about to change all that.

"No. No, we are going to start by getting that motherfucker who took advantage of him."

16. RIGHT AND WRONG

Kate

Today at practice, our guitarist, Travis, wants to do a cover of an old Counting Crows song. I'm starting to feel like Travis has it out for me to fail. Or maybe I'm just so emotional and frustrated today.

I've always loved this music but when Adam Duritz sings, I feel a gorgeous, cool silver, like the edge of a knife is against my skin. It's both perfect and scary. If I let it press too close it will slice me open and all the loneliness and melancholy the music has welled up inside me will spill out onto the floor.

My voice doesn't do the haunting lyrics of "Around Here" justice, and we keep trying it over and over. And over. Until I tell Travis his guitar is off key, he argues, and Layla suggests we all call it a day.

I'm relieved to be done for now, but my body is hurt and hot. Even with the garage door open to let in the cool air, I'm suffocated with so many people around.

"You okay?" Layla presses a bottle of water into my hand.

"Sure. Fine. But he was out of tune. It makes the colors wrong."

"What?"

I need a better filter. Just when I'm sure I might burst into flame, I see Ty by the door. A blast of cool air hits me in the face. "Nothing. I can tell though."

"I'll talk to Travis. He's one of those prickly types who doesn't respond well to change. You're a little prickly yourself. If this is going to work, the two of you will have to figure out how to work out disagreements."

A ball of nerves tumbles inside my stomach. Twisting sensations slosh the water I drank and make me queasy. I know I'm prickly, as Layla puts it, especially since the accident. When you hurt physically all the time, it's hard to be patient with people.

I like it here, though. I've got Ty and Alonzo, and yesterday I even started kicking around a life plan. There are plan B's, sure. I can always go back home, but the look on my mom's face that night, the way I felt every day in that house, it makes it more of a desperate last attempt than a backup plan.

"We'll work it out," I tell Layla.

Ty comes over with an offer of my jacket. "You ready to head out?"

Right. I said I'd go to the gym with him today. Super. "You bet."

Those two little words twist my insides even tighter, make my feet go heavy with dread. I don't want to go to the gym. I don't want to do anything right now, except what we did last time after band practice. That whole foot-rub-and-then-get-naked thing? Yeah, that was fun last week after band practice. I could do that again.

Sweat on my face has turned my hot body cool though, and I'm grateful when he slides his hand into mine and pulls me close. The frosty air makes his breath visible as we walk along.

The quaintness of the town charms me. Evergreen Grove has an energy all its own as we take a moment to breathe in the smells of this little place. Smoke from chimneys, pine from the trees, and the deliciousness of the nearby bakery.

I lean my head against his shoulder, grateful for a moment of quiet. "Hey, so I should be able to start moving into my new place next week. I was thinking I'd go see about some furniture this weekend. Come with me?"

He turns to face me, holding my hand in his as he licks his lips. I know that look. He's thinking of an excuse to get out of it.

"Okay look, if you don't want to go, just say so."

"It's not that I don't want to. Dante said he might have a fight for me. His uncle still referees here and coaches here and there…one of his fighters got injured. It's a small promoter but bigger than any opportunities I've gotten on my own. It's a good opening for me."

My chest hurts. So much is right and wrong in the moment, mixing together in my head. I want this for him, I do. I know it's something he's wanted. I can remember him telling me to wait and see. He would be something big someday.

But I don't need him to be a big deal. I just want *him*. I want him around when I'm tired and hurting. I feel a little selfish but I also know if he starts getting bigger fights, it will take him away from me.

"Hey." He presses his finger to my chin. "You okay? It's a local fight. Only a few hours away. I'd be gone for a day, tops. You could come. We could get a hotel room and celebrate after." He wiggles his eyebrows in comic suggestivity.

"I guess—"

Something flies past my head and smashes through the window of the bakery, making contact with a jarring shatter.

"Holy cow what was that?"

He's shielding me before I can think. A wall of muscle and man, blocking me from running in the direction the object came from or identifying who threw it.

I hit his body with a thud. "Ty, let me go. I can't see anything."

But I already know it's too late. A deep rumble sounds, an engine speeding away down the street. "Don't. Let it go."

"We need to—"

"No worries. I got the plates."

"Good. I wish I'd been able to see who it was. This is a small town. They'd never get away with—"

He puts his hand on my arm. "People are gonna sling trash sometimes, baby. We don't need to get down on their level. Anyway…" He looks through the window where the brick landed. "Looks like everyone's okay."

A group of people have gathered on either side of the entrance, sticking their heads out of the coffee shop door and some looking through the hole in the broken window. Cassie, the girl who runs the shop, runs out to the sidewalk. She's already dialing her phone.

"Did you get the tag number?"

"Yeah. You got a piece of paper?"

She motions for Ty to follow her inside. I hang back behind him, still willing my pulse to shift down out of overdrive.

"Everything okay?" When I turn around, that boxer, Dante, is standing behind me offering a tissue. I didn't realize I'd needed one. Turns out I do.

"Sure. Fine." I point inside unnecessarily. "Ty's inside helping Cassie. They're calling the police I think."

"Good." He nods thoughtfully. "This is a quiet town. Once in a while we get some freaky-ass dust-ups.

Stupid people being stupid. Guess stupid never takes a break, no matter what the weather."

"Guess not." My steps stutter on my way back inside. "Hey, so I heard you got Ty a fight."

He stuffs his hands in his pockets. "If you want to call it that. My uncle had someone fall through and I passed on his name."

Really, I'm happy for Ty. I am. It's just that… "Do you think it's possible to have a relationship while someone like him is in training, or is it, you know, too distracting?"

Because I remember it now and I can't stop remembering. What Terrence said to me. *You'll distract him. You'll keep him from being his best. He already failed because of you.*

"People do all kinds of things."

That's not exactly an answer. Or maybe it is. I look inside, and then back past all the gawking people still looking down the street, as if the truck might come back.

Damn. Judging by everyone's reaction, this was the biggest thing to happen since the rodeo came to town.

Aaand now I'm wondering if they ever have a rodeo in town.

Back inside, bodies mill around the counter where Cassie and Ty are talking. A bewildered young man is sweeping away glass from the table by the window.

I'd been so happy that day. Prom. Ty. Then everything shattered. Like that brick through the window.

Was Terrence right? Maybe I'm not what Ty needs. A local fight I could do, but I can't travel with him across the country if he gets big opportunities. Either he'll leave me behind or he'll hold himself back and lose his career. I know next to nothing about the business, but I'm betting they don't give too many second chances after what happened with that fight he lost.

Ty's coming back outside. I'm detached a little, as he takes my hand, like I'm floating. When he pulls me against his chest, I'm solid again. Suddenly no longer afraid.

Touching him makes me unafraid of everything.

"So maybe today we'll skip the gym," he murmurs into my hair. "Take some food back and take our clothes off."

I let out a whooshing breath. "Will you rub my feet?"

"Will you be naked?"

I bite down on my lips to keep from laughing. "Yes."

"Then I'll warm up the magic fingers. Cassie said the police are coming by, but she'll just give them my number for a statement."

"Oh. Good."

I let him lead the way toward what I've almost come to think of as home these past couple of weeks. Unease winds inside of me, blinks open one eye and then the other as all the misgivings prod it from inside my nervous core.

You don't even know what I've done to get him there, Kate. You're going to ruin everything.

Blurry memories mash together. Me and Ty, talking with our heads together in a quiet corner of the root beer stand back home. Then the dark nightmare, the one that's been visiting me as I drift off to sleep. Terrence telling me I don't deserve his brother, just before he hit the gas and we crashed into a truck head-on.

#

Ty

The night with Kate wasn't as much romance as I'd hoped. I think we were both probably more shaken up by what happened on Main Street than we wanted to admit, and I for one was trying a little too hard to prove it wasn't getting to me.

Not that I can ever know why that brick was thrown. Or at whom. Hard to say, and not worth spending time obsessing over. Except I rolled it over in my mind anyway, wondering if I'd put Kate in danger standing next to her on the street that way. Beating myself up for how I could have, should have done a better job of looking out while we were in public.

We kept our relationship quiet before. Not hidden, exactly, but I worried enough that we didn't exactly hold hands in public. Everyone was broke enough to be equal in Aspiration, but money problems also made people restless. Since living in Evergreen Grove, maybe I got too comfortable.

I'm not comfortable now.

By the time we deal with the vandalism, getting food, and walking Kate back to the B&B, we're starving and exhausted. We eat and I'm about to offer up a foot rub when two nice gentlemen from the County Sherriff's office arrive, because the nice folks in a small town had pointed 'em to where we were for a statement.

One of 'em's the friendly lieutenant who'd let us take Alonzo without booking him, so I make a point of being extra cooperative. Also because I'd been taught growing up to always be extra respectful to law enforcement officers.

Law enforcement, your elders, and women. *Because they can bring you into this world, and they can take you right out.* But definitely law enforcement.

"They're good people doing a hard job," my gran would say about cops. "But you just never know."

Takes a while to get the police to leave. Sierra, who runs the B&B for her aunt, she offers them tea. And scones. Hell, even I stick around for the scones. They're damn good, and not hard enough to break your teeth like some of 'em I'd tried before.

Still. By the time we get around to "How about that foot massage?" Kate conks out less than a minute in. I've KO'd opponents in a street fight who gave up more resistance. One second she's talking to me about getting stuff for her new place, the next she's drooling on the rose-patterned pillow.

I stay the night but don't sleep. Which has been an unfortunate practice a couple—few—times a week. She sleeps fitfully. What she dreams about, I don't know. Whenever I ask, she claims not to remember. In the night though, there's a whole lot of tension in her body. If I lean close, I can hear the soft scrape of her teeth grinding.

Sometimes it's worse. Jerking. One arm shooting out to hit me.

When I lie next to her and rub her back, smooth my fingers along her side, it calms her down. Hell on my night, though. And I thought crashing in Alonzo's basement during a beer pong tournament was bad.

I'm feeling it on Saturday morning when Dante takes me to the floor with an embarrassingly simple throw. "Shit."

"That's twice now. You sick or something?"

Or something. "I'm good. Just tired."

"You've been looking a little worse for wear lately."

I wave off the hand he extends so I can have the dignity of jumping to my feet all on my own. "A few rough nights. I'll be fine."

"You need me to tell Timo you'll take a pass on the fight? We didn't give you much time to prepare."

"Hell no." I get back into position, ready to go again. "Let's do this. I'm fine."

"You know as well as I do, most fighters spend weeks training. No shame in it if you need to—"

"I'm not passing on the fight. I'll be ready. I'm ready now. Just didn't sleep well. I'll go home after this and grab some Z's."

Dante makes a show of turning his head up to a giant clock on the far side of the gym wall. "You've got a bunch of elementary school kids coming in for Tae Kwon Do after this."

Help me now. "So after that."

"Sure. And what about the next time?"

"Next time I'll sleep better." Hard to know if I'm selling this pack of lies when I don't even believe it myself. If I'm sleeping with Kate and she's not sleeping soundly, then neither am I.

Yeah, I could be the guy who gets off and rolls over and lets his girl get through the night however she gets through. I could, except I'd know I was doing it, and my conscience would dog me until I did otherwise.

Anyway, knowing my touch calms her down at night? Knowing I soothe her even when she's sleeping? That's the kind of thing that makes a man feel twenty feet tall.

Dante taps a glove on my shoulder before tossing me a water bottle and climbing out of the ring. "Okay. I'm going to let you get showered and changed for your class. I will say this beforehand, though. Your 'it's complicated' asked me some questions the other day. She's supportive of you doing this, isn't she?"

"Of course she is." The question stops me even though I answer as if I'm certain. Kate was first in line from the time we met, back when we were in school. Before the accident. But a lot about her has changed, and I don't know, it never occurred to me to ask.

Before I can think better of the idea, I tap out a text message:

Hey. You're cool with me doing this fight next week?

It isn't until after I hit send that I think of all the reasons it would've made more sense to wait and ask her in person. Like the fact that she could easily ignore the question, which she seems to be doing.

I stare at the screen until the gym door opens and takes my attention.

"Hey, Mister Tyler!" It's Abbie, one of my adorable little girls, with AJ, of the massive truck that needed glitter.

"Uh, hey." They're early. "I was about to run and change."

"No worries. We're early. Do what you need to do."

"Thanks." I study Abbie, clearly familiar with the place as she runs toward Dante's office to hang up her coat on one of the rows of pegs. Also clear is the fact that Abbie didn't get her light brown skin from her father.

"Hey, so does her mom ever bring her in?" I haven't met the girl's mother so I'm curious.

AJ shrugs. "Abbie's mom lives about a half hour outside of town. She might bring her sometimes, but usually it'll be me or Hayden, my partner. Mostly me."

"Mind if I ask you, if the folks are cool around here?"

He raises his eyebrows. "With me? Or with Abbie?" Rather than wait for my answer, he assumes on his own. "I think mostly, yeah. Not too many people had the balls to say anything. I do have a lot of friends in town and Lieutenant Haas is an old acquaintance, so I have someone I can call if there's ever an issue. Not to mention I'd rip apart anyone who threatened my little girl."

"Yeah. Of course." Suddenly I respect the man and his glitter truck a whole lot more.

He swallows, shaking off the serious and flashing a big smile. "But hey. Sure, I've had my issues. I don't have to tell you that a kid can't stay insulated from those. We all do our best, that's all."

"Right." I clear my throat. "So I'm gonna run and change so I can teach your daughter now."

"We sure do appreciate it."

He gives me a wave and a bright smile and I walk away, wondering why I even asked the question. One I mostly knew the answer to, and one where the answer had little bearing on me, anyway.

Unless I think things with Kate might get a lot more serious in the future. I never hoped for a family of my own, or even settling down. Lately I find myself wondering if I could get there someday. Or am I hoping for too much?

Maybe I'm just so damn tired I'm starting to go a little crazy. "Need a damn nap," I mutter as I head for the locker rooms.

17. REALITY TV

Kate

I lean forward carefully in my chair, desperately seeking nachos. I'm with Alonzo at Joe's, a cute little bar and grill type place that I've heard has the best appetizers in the area. Not that it would be a difficult contest to win with all of three food establishments in town, but I'm psyched to try them out. If nothing else, I'm enjoying the ambiance of random music-related wall hangings and the festive-looking, multicolored Christmas lights that give the room a certain warmth in spite of us being well past the holidays.

"Uh, do you see our waiter?"

"He'll be here," Alonzo grumbles.

Alonzo's groaning quietly with a frosty ginger ale pressed to his forehead. "Damn. Some days I actually feel shitty enough to think I'll never drink again."

My back's been killing me today and I can't take more ibuprofen until I eat some food. "Isn't 'I'll never drink again' the thing you chant to yourself while you're tossing your cookies?"

"Only sometimes." He lowers the glass with a grimace and takes a sip.

"Loaded nachos, no jalapeno." A handsome bartender named Jake sets down a massive plate on the tiny table between us.

"Oh. Hell. Yeah." Alonzo pinches his fingers together. "Might still be a little drunk. Need to soak up the leftover alcohol."

I moan around the mouthful of fried salt and cheese. "Okay, maybe I'm just tired and hungry but these are definitely good."

You know two people are starving when they haven't seen each other in days and yet they're too busy scarfing their food to talk. It takes some time before we slow down, Alonzo finally relinquishing the white-knuckle grip on his glass, and me feeling full enough to take something for my pain.

"God. I'm trying to keep this promise I made to Ty that I wouldn't take any prescription-strength painkillers and it's kind of miserable." As I say this, I shift in my chair and then shift again, trying to find a comfortable position.

Alonzo lifts his head. "See, that's one more reason it's lucky Ty and I never dated. He's got all these crazy puritanical rules I could never adhere to."

"And yet you dated his twin brother."

Alonzo snorts. "Yeah. Ty and I don't talk about that."

"Oh come on. He knows, right?"

Alonzo shrugs. "I'm sure he does. I don't think he approved."

"He couldn't have disapproved. You guys are still friends."

Another shrug. "I don't bring it up. He doesn't either. Our friendship works so long as we don't discuss anything personal that involves feelings. Last time I did, he shoved me into the kitchen counter. Anyway, so how's tricks with you? Sounds like you're keeping your nose clean. That's good."

I wrinkle said nose, worried. Alonzo's made his concern for me clear since Terrence was killed in that car wreck. Well, the longer I'm in Evergreen Grove, the more I'm nervous for *him*. It wasn't clear to me from social media and email just how much he partied. How promiscuous he is. And far be it from me to deny anyone a good time, but there's a reckless edge to his behavior that scares me.

Getting arrested? Still being drunk when we meet for dinner? That's serious. "Alonzo, maybe you guys do need to talk. You deserve to resolve things with Ty if you have things left unsaid."

Says the girl who's still afraid to ask about their official relationship status.

He shakes his head. "Nah. It's not my issue. Ty's not over Terrence's death. Neither am I, if I'm being honest, but of all people, it's not his job to help me work out my shit."

"But—"

"Enough about me. How are things with you?"

I put down my fork in the middle of scooping beans onto a chip. "You know that TV show where a person gets put under a sleeping curse, and then after that whenever they fall asleep, they wind up in a room full of fire?"

"You know I mostly watch sports and reality TV if I watch anything at all. I like the really twisted shit like the one about strange sex fetishes or sex that got people put in the ER. Or if you take the wayback machine, this girl I was seeing for a minute had a video tape of this show about a bunch of rich girls trying to date a dude in the Australian Outback. I mean, is that messed up or what? They're all camping in the wilderness and one of the contestants is looking for a place to plug in her curling iron."

"I don't know what's worse. The idea that a minute is probably your longest recent relationship or that she had reality TV shows saved to VHS."

"The video thing. Trust me. She had boxes and boxes of them. Didn't want to replace all her shit, she said."

I sigh. "Okay. Fine. Anyway, I binge-watched so much stuff after the accident, all the shows are running together for me now. But the thing is, I couldn't remember the accident. For the longest time, I couldn't remember anything. For a few weeks, after my short-term memory was even spotty in little ways, like I'd realize I had something in my hand but didn't remember picking it up."

"Hell, girl. I call that Tequila Tuesday."

"Well, I can't blame day drinking."

"Right. Continue."

"Anyway, I've been remembering. Maybe it's being around Ty, I don't know. Now I'm having nightmares. I'm worried about telling Ty because he'll want to know about the accident and…I just don't know if I'm ready to tell him."

Alonzo stiffens. "Why? What about the accident?"

I put a hand over Alonzo's. "Not about you. Not about Ty. About me. Something Terrence said…right before it happened."

"Well what the hell did he say?"

This was a bad idea. Alonzo is someone I've always found easy to talk to, and in spite of his frequent imbibing, he tends to give good advice. But I'm talking about Terrence right now, and I can see that all of his usual ease has left his body.

"He told me…" I look around. Stupidly, perhaps. It's not like Ty should be in here now. He told me he'd be at the gym all afternoon and evening. But saying something with the exact wrong person standing behind me is exactly the sort of thing I'd do.

Alonzo slaps his other hand over mine. "Don't do this to me, girl. What did he say?"

"He told me I wasn't good enough for Ty. That I didn't deserve him, and I was going to ruin his career."

Alonzo sits back in his chair. He looks thoughtful. What he does *not* look is surprised.

"You knew." I lean forward, getting in his face as much as our postage-stamp-sized table and a plate of loaded nachos will let me. "You knew he felt that way. Why in the hell didn't you ever clue me in? Why didn't Ty?"

Alonzo springs to life in spite of his hangover. "I thought he'd change his mind. You were a sweet kid. You'd grow on him. Anyway, they had a fight a couple of weeks before…you know. The wedge had already been driven in good and tight. Why make it worse?"

The part he doesn't say, but I know without needing to ask? Alonzo's loyalty was to Terrence first, no matter how much he might have liked me at the time.

"God." I shove my chair out and slap a twenty dollar bill on the table to cover my food. "I have to go."

"Kate. Come on. Wait."

I don't wait for him to follow, but a few seconds after the cold wind outside slaps me in the face and I start down the wooden stairs from Joe's second-floor location, Alonzo's hustling behind me.

"Kate. Seriously. Stop a second."

In my fury I keep going, and that's shitty, but I feel shitty, too. I pass Delia's, downstairs from Joe's and still looking messed up with a quickie patch job on the front window. Up the block, I head in the direction I need to walk to get to the B&B, although when I pass in front of Roy's gym, I stop.

"Oof." Alonzo runs into my back. "Thanks for the warning, girl."

"Like the warning I got before Terrence trapped me in a car, and went off on how I wasn't good enough for his brother?"

"Yeah, okay. That's fair."

I don't respond because I'm busy paying attention to something else. Ty's across the street inside the gym, bowing to a handful of tiny people in white uniforms. They bow back. It's kind of the most adorable thing I've ever seen.

"Do you agree?" After watching Ty with the kids for a few minutes—he's good with them—I chance a glance back at Alonzo.

"About what Terrence said?" He gives me a look. "Please. I loved that guy, but I'll be the first to admit he had some issues. He let those issues color his viewpoint like we all do. It sucks that he didn't give you a chance, but I think if he had lived, he would've realized how great you are, like the rest of us."

"Thanks." Except I'm not sure that he isn't the one who caused the accident. And I can't say anything, because I don't know for sure. I may never know. Plus, it would kill Ty and Alonzo both.

"He's going for it though. You know that, right? That fight he lost right before Terrence died, it's eaten at him for all this time." Alonzo nods at the window. "He's been drifting since he lost you both. This is good for him."

"I know. I'm happy for him. Honest. Hey. So I was thinking I might finally enroll in college." I give Alonzo a smile that's probably way too big, but Alonzo's busy checking out an off-duty firefighter heading up the steps to Joe's and doesn't seem to notice.

"Something about that turnout gear," he mumbles.

It's true, what I said. I *am* happy for Ty. It's just that the more I think about what Terrence said, the more I worry he was right. After all, he felt strongly enough to have this big talk with me that day. Maybe I'm really not the right person for Tyler Thacker, not if he's going to be the champion he deserves to be.

"He deserves to know. You know that, right? It's not so much what Terrence said but the fact that you're keeping a secret. Secrets come between two people faster than anything. Trust me."

"You're right. I'll tell him." I will. After his next fight. He deserves not to be distracted before then. Right now, he deserves all the focus to be on him.

He does. Terrence was right. He deserves everything.

#

Ty

I'm fighting a guy named Roland Cadiz. We're pretty equally matched as far as size, but from what I've seen on his tapes, he's fast and his ground game is ugly.

"You've got this," Dante tells me. "He may be fast and he fights dirty, but you're precise with your strikes. Go in decisive and take him down early."

"Right. Sounds good." Sounds great. Too bad I'm already on my second energy drink and I'm not feeling as energized as the label says I ought to be.

It's all good though. I'll get in there and we'll bump chests at weigh-in. We'll snarl and face off at the start of the fight and the adrenaline will surge. I'll be good.

And I am. We get in the ring, we touch gloves. I see him favoring his right leg so I go for a sweep. It doesn't take him down, but it throws him off.

In between blocking his shots, I alternate throwing jabs at his face and trying to weaken that leg. For a little while, it's looking good. He's looking like that leg won't hold him much longer and that last shot I got to his temple left him dazed.

We make it through one round and then another. Holding my own, buzzing on the high of the fight.

It only takes a second to turn things around.

Early in the third, my exhaustion catches up with me and I let my arm drop at the wrong moment. A right hook jars my senses. The rapid follow-up has blood trickling into my eye. I can't see out of my left side.

If the official notices how bad it is, he'll probably call the fight. At most I've got a minute or two left to make something happen.

He taunts with a slicing gesture, trying to say "You're a dead man."

I bite down on my mouth guard and give him the finger.

Then I throw another jab. It's a sloppy shot to the body and I'm embarrassed by it, so I push forward and get in close enough to throw an uppercut. He grabs me around the middle and it's ugly then, but I keep on throwing body blows until he loosens up. The second he does, I go hard with a knee to his inner thigh.

This time he goes down. Miracle of miracles.

I swear this must be the stuff of Kate's nightmares if she hasn't given up and left the audience by now. I'm down here on the mat with this guy slipping and sliding in both our blood, grappling to get a good enough hold to make him stay down.

He keeps trying to choke me with his legs, which can be the kiss of death. Lucky thing I'm too slippery for him to hold.

I get him pinned before the buzzer sounds, down on the mat with my arm around his throat. He's fighting the chokehold, but I've got him dead and he finally taps out.

The sounds around me fade out as they announce my win, doing the obligatory song and dance before someone gets me an ice pack and sits me down for stitches. Guaranteed my face has looked prettier than it does today.

"Damn," Dante says when we meet up after. "You were trying hard to earn your street cred, weren't you?"

"He was a street fighter for years before this. He's got plenty of street cred." That's Kate, leveling me with a look I can't read. She doesn't look pissed but she isn't exactly happy.

Whatever's going on in her head, it dials down the excitement of my win a few notches. It's not like my happiness rises and falls with her, but if she's not happy for me then it does take the edge off the thrill. But then she smiles broadly and hugs me, so maybe I imagined the look I saw before.

"Great fight," she murmurs in my ear. "Terrence would be proud."

"Yeah. I think so, too." I sure hope so, anyway. Last time we talked, we had a fight about how he thought

I was throwing it all away. More than anything I wish he could be here, and I do wish he'd be proud.

I hug her again. "Thanks for being here, baby. I want us to go out to dinner tomorrow. To celebrate. And we'll go out and look for stuff for your place since I wasn't able to do it before now."

She gives me a smile but a smaller one than before. I want to ask if everything's okay, but I've got Dante coming down the hall before I have a chance.

"Hey," he says. "You and I should talk."

Kate's making her retreat before I have a chance to ask her to wait. It's okay. She and I can talk after things have died down.

"Definitely," I say as we make our way to the dressing rooms. "I think I'm ready to sit down and tell you the full deal about my brother. Lay it all out. See if it can help your case."

"That's great. Thank you." He pushes inside the locker room and waits for me to follow. "But there's something else." He points to the spot above my eye. "Five stitches?"

My hand is almost at the spot before I stop myself. "Man, you know how these things go. Cuts and scrapes happen. Besides, I won."

"You won by the skin of your nose. Now listen. I'm the last guy in the world to tell you to put your career before your girl. Someone tried that with my Michelle and I told them to fuck off. That said, I also retired from boxing a short while after we met. I won't pretend to know what's going on right now, but if the girl's keeping you up at night, you'd better find a solution."

I take a hard breath and then push it down, trying to calm myself before I do something stupid. I know

Dante doesn't have anything against Kate, but I'm beginning to wonder what's going on. Alonzo's warned me off of her. Terrence did, before he died. I know damn well her mother didn't want us together.

Are she and I completely doomed to fail? Am I screwed if I try to have my fight career and Kate, too?

"I know," Dante says. "You probably want to take a swing at me right now. I don't blame you. All I ask is that you give it some real thought first. Honest to God, I'm trying to help you, here. I don't want your heart broken or hers."

With the feeling of my heart sliding down to the concrete floor, I give him a short nod. "I'll think it over."

18. MAGICAL SPOT

Kate

This is the most I've dreaded seeing Ty, ever.

Even that night when he and Alonzo tracked me down in South Carolina, I was shocked to see him but it wasn't the worst thing ever. Tonight? Tonight dread wraps around me, squeezing tight, like a constrictor.

We decided we'd meet back here at the B&B after the fight, instead of splurging on a hotel. I rode back the forty-five minute drive with one of my new bandmates, but Tyler had to wrap things up with officials and whatnot before he could leave. Neither of us were sure what time he'd be finished, only that he promised to pick up something at a drive-through on the way.

Couldn't be the least bit hungry.

I need to relax or I'll never get through the night. I've lost feeling in my right leg thanks to the car trip, not to mention the tension of the fight. Who would have thought that twenty minutes in a person's life could be so bloody and awful?

Ty never got banged up so much when he fought in that gravel lot back home. Not even with the big guys.

For the first time in days, I succumb to the pressure and dig through my backpack, pulling out a bottle of little white pills. While the stack of exercise papers from the PT hasn't gotten as much play as it ought to have, I've been working on some of the relaxation stuff Ty told me about, and not crutching on the prescription pills so much. It's both a point of pride and irony that it was Ty who helped me to decrease my reliance on them, and Ty who's got me so nervous I feel I need one now.

Along with the muscle relaxer, I break into the little bottle of champagne that was in the mini fridge when I first checked in, still untouched. Waiting for a romantic night I guess, but anxiety and a nice brut pair just as well, don't they?

I'm in the shower, letting the hot water give my tight neck and shoulders a pounding when I hear him.

"You shouldn't leave your door unlocked. Anyone could come in."

I smile to myself, but sadness balloons in my chest. "That was sort of the point."

"You wanted strangers walking in the room?"

"More like I knew you were coming, and I wanted to take a shower so I figured you could let yourself in."

A large, quite naked man steps into my shower. "You thought right."

"Sometimes I get lucky," I murmur.

He's already kissing me. Excited, feverish kisses along my neck and jaw. My lips. A commanding tongue, hot with purpose, slips inside before I even think to stop him.

I should say something. Now, before things go too far. I should. I can't.

"I won tonight," he whispers in my ear. His body slides against mine and clear evidence of his arousal probes between my thighs.

Excitement all around, and I can't say my body's immune.

Just this once. One last time.

I could stop him. I could push him away and tell him to wait because I have something to say, and so could begin the downward spiral of our night, but I'm selfish. I don't want to fight. Not yet, not ever.

"Kate, it's because of you, you know? Knowing you were there gave me the strength."

I push away the pang in my chest and focus on his lips and hands on my chest. I let him have his way because I want it, too. Because fighting him would be harder and this is one fight I actually want to lose.

He reaches outside the curtain for a condom. "Tell me if anything hurts."

I shake my head. For one thing, I've taken drugs. For another, this is going to be our last time together. He could break my arms and legs and I wouldn't complain.

If it weren't so fucked up, I'd see the humor in how it required extreme sorrow to not mind things hurting me physically quite so much. The muscle relaxer should kick in soon, but just having him here to touch me makes the pain less.

He starts out slow and gentle, which isn't at all how I'd pictured this would go. We're in a shower, after all. Standing. There's a mac-daddy showerhead and a wall with pretty tiles. This is the place where pretty movie ingénues get to have sex, not plain Janes like me.

I'll tell him. I will. *After.*

"Ty. Harder."

"I don't want to hurt you."

"You can't hurt me." *You can't hurt me because I'm already dying inside. I can't keep you, so I'm going to remember this for as long as I can.*

He lifts me, pressing against the cool tile and driving forward like I'm one of his opponents and he's trying to run me into the chain-link. The little dish full of toiletries gets in the way of his elbow, spilling soap and hair conditioner at our feet.

I'd care but I'm too busy wrapping my legs around his waist. "Is this okay?"

"That's good. Tighter. Angle your hips. Right there."

I take a handful of his shoulder in the fingers of my right hand. Pain arcs through me when I realize I won't be doing this again.

"I'm close," he whispers.

Under the spray of the water I barely hear it, but it's there. His declaration, but also a question. He won tonight and he's still here, asking for permission, because that's who he is.

I'm not close, but I didn't expect to be. Too much anxiety, plus the drugs. Too much fear.

Until he hooks one arm under my butt to keep holding me and uses the other hand to strum between my legs, igniting sparks of pleasure.

"I'm close," he says again. "You close?"

"I am now." I almost chuckle, but it isn't funny. Just…well, okay. A little funny.

He thrusts harder, angling his hips. I shout out when he manages to hit some magical spot, the likes of which I've only read about in magazines and assumed was fictional.

Before I know it I'm crying, shaking and burying my face in his neck. "God, Ty. Oh, God." All I can do is say his name over and over. I've lost the power of any other kind of speech. I'm so stunned I don't even seem to notice or mind when he doesn't ask at the end how it was.

Of course not. He already knows.

"Here, baby. Let me get you a towel."

He grabs one for me and one for himself, shutting down the water and climbing out. We get dried off in silence, me because I know what I'm about to say, and I'm not sure why for him until he speaks.

"I've got burgers out there on the bedside table. I hope that's okay."

"Sure. Thanks. You didn't have to do that though."

"You bet your ass I did. Needed a break from chicken breasts for one night."

"Oh. Okay."

"Everything all right? If you're tired, we can go to bed right after we eat."

God, this hurts. This is so painful I want to knock myself out so I don't have to be here for any of it.

"I'm all right. But, uh. Hang on…" I grab one of the robes that came with the room when I checked in. I don't want to take the time and awkwardness of getting dressed but I don't want to be naked for this.

Okay. "So. Um. I was thinking we should talk."

His smile is its usual warm self, but I see the uncertainty. "Talk, huh? 'We should talk' usually doesn't mean anything good."

"I don't…" I don't know what to say. Honestly I didn't expect that I'd be attached again. When he and Alonzo showed up at that party, I was so mad at them for interrupting my life, and now this *is* my life. Him and me and this sleepy town that doesn't stress me out nearly so much as living back home.

He pulls on a pair of pants and I breathe a sigh that at least he's partially clothed. "Okay. What did you want to talk about?"

I draw a deep breath, but I've stalled for as long as I can. "I think maybe we shouldn't see each other anymore. The way we have been. You know."

My assumption was that he'd be disappointed. Or maybe neutral. Let's be honest, we haven't been seeing each other that long, and I don't even know if he's seeing anyone else right now. I never asked.

He's angry though, and that's a scenario I didn't see coming.

He stalks forward, stopping just in front of me with his face twisted in bitterness. "No. I'm not so sure I do. Why don't you explain it to me?"

#

Ty

"What in the hell is this about, Kate?"

I'm pacing. Restless. Punching my fist into my hand, which is a dumb move considering I already pummeled a man's hard skull tonight and my fist is not real happy. For real though, I can't make sense of this right now.

I thought things were just starting to get good. It was like old times, but better because we weren't the same stupid kids. Or so I thought.

We were having fun spending time together. Weren't we?

"Is this because I didn't have time to go shopping with you? I told you after the fight—"

"It's got nothing to do with shopping. I don't care about shopping."

I cross my arms over my chest and look at her.

"Okay, I care a little about shopping but really it's not—Ty, I want you to have your dreams. I'm just not sure there's a place for me in there."

I get up in her face. Too fast and too aggressive, but I'm pissed and not willing to take this answer without an explanation. "That doesn't make a damn bit of sense. You're mine and I've had you in my plan every step of the way. Even when I didn't want to. Senior year of high school when you were too young to date, I still kept an eye on you. I waited until you were old enough to take to the prom. I *waited* because you were part of my *mother-fucking plan*!"

"Shh." She waves her hands and looks at the door, nervous. "I don't want to get kicked out of here. You're entitled to your feelings, but do not get me in trouble. Please."

I make a noise with my tongue and show her my back. I'm too angry to look at her. "Sure. I'll stay over here and fume quietly. You know what? Fuck you, Kate. You don't get to tell me how to experience my anger."

"You're right. I'm sorry. I'm doing this all wrong."

"The fact that you're doing it at all is wrong."

I hear the depth of her inhale from across the room. "You've been exhausted lately, I can tell. You leave in the morning before I'm awake so I won't notice, but I know you're not sleeping when you stay here at night."

Well, hell. Busted. "I sleep."

She wraps her robe tighter around her legs as she sits on the bed. I was just inside this girl. Why is she smoothing her robe over her legs like she needs more coverage?

"I have nightmares from the accident. At first I didn't realize they might be affecting you, but I've been remembering more things and I can tell—a couple of times when you weren't here I woke in the middle of struggling. With the pillows and blankets. With myself. You can't have what you and Terrence planned out for the future and have me, too. Not until I get rid of the nightmares."

My heart beats harder than I've been able to feel it since my brother died. Since I thought I might have lost Kate for good. I'm aware of it hammering in my chest, and the sensation of a giant vice squeezing the everloving shit out of it.

"The dream Terrence and I had involved the both of us. No matter what happens, I'm never having my dream." I spit the words at her. Rage shakes my insides and I'm not sure where to even direct it.

Dammit, if I didn't love this girl, I'd want to punch the look of pity off her face.

"He wanted you to have it all, Ty. He told me you were a better fighter than he could ever hope to be and you just needed the right recognition. That someday you'd get to the top. He was *right*, Ty. I saw it tonight, how great you are. Even as tired as you were. But you barely won and what if next time you're not so lucky? I'm going to hold you back."

"Baby, luck had nothing to—" Wait. "When did you talk to my brother about my career?"

I'd introduced them, sure. They'd talked. But they hadn't exactly hung out and swapped cookie recipes.

"The day I was supposed to meet you at the mall to get your tux for prom."

Ice cold washes me from head to toe. "You mean the day of the accident."

She nods. I approach the bed and notice the moisture running down her cheeks, two silent rivers that she's making no motion to hide or wipe away.

I reach for her hand. "Baby. You said you didn't remember."

"I didn't. And then once I could… Now I can't forget."

I close my eyes. For a minute I don't say a word. I'm tempted to urge them open, dry her tears, and take her to bed. Make us both forget. Terrence is dead and whatever happened is in the past. But it's gonna hang over us. The not knowing will eat at me.

It's already eating her.

"I know we had some differences of opinions. Whatever he said—"

She stands up so fast her head almost hits my chin. "He said he'd sacrificed too much for you to get your ass handed to you over some cheap piece of pussy. He said I made you weak, I distracted you, and I was only going to drag you down."

She's crying harder now. I want to take her in my arms. I want to hit something. I want to go back in time and tell Terrence to live his own damn life.

"Baby—"

"No. He was right, Ty. You're not weak, he had that dead wrong but…God. I *love* you. You deserve your dream. I know he pulled strings to get you that fight with ZZ Marques back then. Being with me kept you from training enough the first time and it almost did again. How many fights can you lose before you don't get another chance? I definitely won't have it be my fault, or else you'll resent me. Please."

She's balled herself up. Closed off. I want to argue and yell. I want to tell her she's wrong, but I'm also remembering my brother and the things he said.

You have no idea what I had to give up for that fight. How could you blow it the way you did?

"Did Terrence say something to you about the fight?"

"It doesn't matter."

She's wrong. Terrence was wrong. "Kate. Terrence was wrong. That fight my brother got so mad at me for losing, it had nothing to do with you."

The catch of her breath pulls at my throat. "And this one?"

Hell "It doesn't matter. I still won."

She nods slowly. "I hope so. If you come up with a way not to fight on borrowed time, you let me know. In the meantime, we should take a break. And you should get some rest."

My fingers curl into fists. She's talking crazy. I don't want to take a break. Look what happened to us last time? One misunderstanding and years went by without us even speaking to each other.

"Kate, no."

Heavy weights pull at my eyelids. I really am exhausted. Even more so now that I've been held up from settling into the super comfortable king this room has.

"So much is going to change if your career takes off. Things we'll need to figure out. But we're never going to get there at all if we don't take a step back from this. Don't you think?"

My knuckles crack when I flex my fingers. "No. I don't think. I don't want some kind of break. Temporary breaks become permanent break-ups, Kate. No. No way. We aren't doing that."

"Ty, please."

"I said *no.* Baby, I don't want to fight with you. But if you tell me to walk out that door, don't expect me to come back."

I picture my gran fanning herself over how stupid and stubborn I'm being. Can't be helped. Even if her intentions are good, the way Kate is trying to push me out to sea when I'd finally found safe harbor in my life again has got me ready to swing first and ask questions never.

"Then let's not fight." She's not saying it though like everything's okay. Sorrow and resolve pull her pretty features toward the floor. "Look, I just got to Evergreen Grove. I like it here. I want to stay. And you're about to leave. Which is probably, hopefully, if things go well, going to happen a lot. I don't know how this all works between us."

I've got no answer for her. Dante told me if my next fight goes well, I'll probably be offered bigger bouts. I could travel all over the world. And I do hate to leave Kate when I just got her back. This dream is what I've always wanted though.

Dammit. I don't have an answer. "We'll figure something out."

She's still crying. "All I'm asking for is some space to do that on my own first."

I grab my wallet and shoes. "That's really what you want? You're sure?" Searing, burning rips through my chest. There she goes, ripping that piece of my heart out again.

She stands up in front of me and runs her thumb along the side of my face, right next to the cut over my eye. “After all those stitches? Yeah. I’m sure.”

“You know sending me out the door doesn’t guarantee I’ll never need stitches again.”

“I’m doing my best here, Ty.”

I turn away and stuff my feet into my shoes. Turning back, I start to say more and then stop. I’m not gonna stand here and beg.

I take long strides toward the bed and then back again before something I can’t control takes over and I let loose a growl, sweeping every ornament and knickknack off the top of the pretty, tasteful dresser.

“Like I said. You ask me to leave, don’t expect me to come back.”

“Ty…I’m sorry.”

“Yeah. I’m sure you are.”

19. TWO BROTHERS AND A BILLY GOAT

Ty

My gloves are fraying, I've pounded the bag so much this morning. Dante unlocked the door and let me go to work while he went to do paperwork in his office. Everything's a blur since then. Hitting circuits of speed bag, treadmill, speed rope and now the heavy bag has done nothing—less than nothing—to bleed off the anger trapped inside me.

I feel like a pressure cooker, and any minute now I'm gonna splatter the mess of myself all over the walls.

"Shoulda damn well seen this coming." After all, it technically isn't the first time she's sent me away. Yeah, her mother may have done it the last time, but how many times did she reach out to find me after that?

Is what we have together really so weak that she'd let my dead brother sway her opinion?

My legs ache from the position I've been holding, but the burn of my muscles is nothing compared to the burn inside my chest. I'm trying to remember back to when I felt all dead in there and when I thought that wasn't preferable.

A sudden movement draws me up, stopping me before I hit Dante square in the chest. He's gotten in my face, right in front of the heavy bag.

"Bold move, man."

"I've taken hits before, my friend. Had to snap you out of it somehow."

He pats me on the shoulder the way I think a father would. Hard to really assess since he's only got a couple of years on me and I didn't have any kind of father growing up, but it's got enough of that feel that I find myself looking away before I get any kind of feelings about it.

I press my lips together so hard my teeth ache. "I didn't need to stop. I'm too keyed up right now."

"Yeah." He leans himself on a massive rolled-up floor mat that's been pushed against the wall. "What I think is you had a fight with your girl and you're in here looking to put the hurt on something else. Don't think I haven't done it myself."

My arm shoots out, giving a hard and painful slap to the heavy bag. "Man, you need to stop acting like you know me. Just because we both came into contact with the same damn sicko—"

"Arlo Specter is a cancer." Dante's face turns to stone. He's always been outgoing and friendly. Like me.

You open more doors with a smile, my gran always said. I've always tried to be friendly. Terrence never bothered. Sometimes I wonder if it's worthwhile.

Dante's staring me down like we're ready to go head to head in the octagon, and he plans to make sure I bleed. "I wasn't the one he… You know."

"Yeah. I do know." Dante sucks in a breath. "I also know I spent years—*years*—even after I got free of his influence, being an angry piece of shit who used people and lied and medicated with drugs and alcohol. It's a wonder I lived this long, given the way I played fast and loose with my own life. So I'm thinking there's a good chance your brother died thanks to the things that happened to him, and that's something you need to resolve.

You're not angry at your girl. You don't hate me or yourself. Focus on who's to blame here, and then let's get to the work of fighting back."

"The thing is..." I press my fists together, my chest burning. "He pulled away. We got separated after a while in foster care, and instead of telling me what was going on, he blamed Kate. He made it all about me being too distracted with a girl, when he was screwing his coach to get me fights. I didn't want his damn help!"

The heavy bag swings and I realize I've hit it again. Dante reaches out to steady the thing, then gets in my face.

"Specter was good at finding what people needed and using it as leverage. He used my mother. She had medical bills. I owed him for years. With your brother, if it hadn't been you, it would've been something else. I never had a brother, but I know it was a hard day for me when my father found out, and that was years later. I'd bet anything in the world he was ashamed to admit to you what was going on. Blaming your girl was easier."

I stand on legs I can barely feel. Without comment, Dante passes me a gym towel to wipe off my face, which is ugly and sweaty from my meltdown.

"She listened though, man. The car wreck that killed him, she was in the passenger seat. She was supposed to meet me but I guess he took her for a ride and told her she needed to let me go have my dream. She dumped me after I won the fight. Said Terrence was right. How twisted up is that? It isn't my dream without her."

He's looking at me. Silently. It's freaking me out.

"Come on, man, now you're giving me silence?"

This guy's had an opinion about everything from my stances to the color of my socks since I met him.

"You're not going to like it."

"Just say it."

"I think it sounds like she loves you a lot."

"Are you serious right now?"

Dante chuckles and paces a few steps before turning back. "It's like this. You ask anyone at that fight, they'll tell you it looked like you were about to get creamed. All that blood going into your eye. I don't know how you could even see. You were fading fast in the third round and even my mom watching at home knew. She's got dementia by the way, so she doesn't actually know dick about anything. You see my point."

I make a noise under my breath, but I decide not to argue. "Yeah, I see what you're trying to say."

"You told me you haven't been sleeping well. Your girl doesn't sleep well. I don't know, but I'm betting she has nightmares after your brother died right next to her in that accident. Can't imagine what it's like for her every night, but I can damn sure make a call about what it was like seeing you in that fight. I'd have dumped your ass, too."

"Geez—fuck!" It's a struggle to get my gloves off when I'm shaking with so much adrenaline. When I finally manage to rip them open with my teeth, they hit a wall halfway across the room.

"Here." Dante motions for me to follow him. "Someone I want you to meet."

We trek over to Delia's, where AJ is wearing a toolbelt and gloves, directing a couple of guys as they replace the glass in the window. He waves and goes back to his task, luckily too fast to notice I didn't return the gesture.

"So he does construction or something?"

"Actually, he sort of runs a shelter here in town for people who need a place to stay. Mostly women and children who have been in difficult situations. Also kind of earned himself a rep as the town handyman. You know how it is. Someone learns you have a skill and everyone's suddenly asking you for help."

"Hey, guys." Cassie walks past and hands over a couple of coffee cups, barely breaking her stride as she goes to talk to a tall man in a peacoat near the register.

"Another upside," Dante says with a smile. "You don't have to actually order ever again when you come into Delia's. Now, over this way."

He leads the way to a table near the back where someone's set up a mini lending library by the condiment station, and two older men are sitting at the table perusing the offerings.

"Ay bendito, what is this one? The title suggests perhaps a story about military training but there is a woman tied with rope on the cover." The older man hands it to his friend, a younger guy wearing a T-shirt that reads "Two Brothers and a Billy Goat" where the goat is mixing tunes on an old-school turntable setup.

Goat-guy pushes the book back. "It's a good book. Don't judge before you give it a try. Also, don't read it in public."

Dante makes an uncomfortable noise. "Ernesto, please stop pushing erotica on my uncle. I can't tell you how uncomfortable that is."

Okay. Awkward.

I cough and point to the shirt. "My friend Alonzo has that shirt."

The younger guy smiles. "Saw them spin at a club in Charlotte a few months ago. Good house music."

Wouldn't surprise me if Alonzo'd been to that same show. He practically makes a career out of partying.

Dante pulls out a chair and gestures for me to sit. Before I do, I turn to him for explanation.

"So these clowns here," Dante gestures to the two men and their romance novels, "are going to help you out."

"Help me with what?"

"I can't be your trainer. I don't have the time to travel, and really if you think about it, it's not a good fit."

"What do you mean? It's a great fit."

"I'm too close to what happened to your brother. It's personal for me, what does or doesn't happen to your career. You need someone who's focused on helping you succeed and not their own agenda.

"Now. I'm still here any day of the week to help you, man, but as much as I want to, I can't travel to every fight. But my uncle Timo here," he points to the older one, "he's been working with this organization called RingFoundation that's working to take the corruption and whatnot out of boxing and MMA. Ernesto here is a retired member of the group who's looking to get into athlete management. Be the change and all that. I think he'd be perfect for you."

I examine Ernesto. He's in his thirties or maybe young forties if I'm guessing accurately. Friendly and quiet. Some fighters have big personalities, like Dante. Some are more subdued, like me. I can see Ernesto is still in shape, not tall but built for power. In spite of a handsome face, a few bumps indicate broken bones. Nose and maybe a cheekbone.

"So what's your story?"

"I got paid to go down. They pulled me off the streets. Undefeated for weeks running in a moving street-fighting ring. Needed the money for my sister. Then they offered me a huge purse, threatened my sister, but I only got the purse if I took a hit. He rubs at his cheek, under a prominent scar. "I'll train you well, though. Swear."

"I believe you." I fought on the streets. You learn your best moves when there's no referee. Then I turn to Dante, my emotions torn after the last twenty-four hours. "What would you do?"

"This one has to be up to you. Thing is, you made a wise move getting out of that fight against ZZ Marques back then. You should never have been in that ring, and fighters have died going up against someone they weren't ready for. Maybe you had the skills to take him on, but Specter didn't know you well enough. Truth was he probably didn't care. If you really want to be a champion, don't do it for what your brother wanted, do it for you and do it the right way." He gestured around the table. "These guys know about the corruption and lack of oversight in the sport. They can help keep an eye on you and keep you safe."

Keep me safe. Like Kate wanted.

Even Terrence never mentioned my safety. He wanted me to win, and I get why. But my winning was about him.

I nod and shake hands with Dante's people, thanking them both for coming. "Let me think about it," I tell them.

I walk home to Alonzo's in nothing but workout shorts and a sweatshirt, welcoming the cold to clear my head. I have an awful lot of thinking to do.

#

Kate

"It was nice of you to show me around campus."

It turns out Ollie the physical therapist is also a volunteer firefighter in Evergreen Grove. I bumped into him on my way back from band rehearsal one afternoon while he and some guys were washing their big red truck. I asked if he'd give me a tour of the campus sometime.

This morning, he'd texted me and kindly mentioned he had a few hours free. I told him if he knew me better, he'd never text me on a weekday morning and expect me to be lucid, but then I remembered I was working on being a real, live, functioning human being so I sent him another text and told him I'd meet him if he could please have coffee waiting.

I brought coffee with me just in case.

I haven't seen Ty in a week. Not since the night I so gracelessly said goodbye.

Every time I go to Alonzo's house, my chest hurts, a squeezing, flailing, fluttering feeling that both begs for him to be there so I can see him and hopes to God he'll be absent. It's always the latter, and I miss him like crazy.

It's getting harder to tell myself that I did the right thing. Especially when I picture the hurt and disbelief on his face.

Fingers snap in front of my face. "Earth to Kate. Can you hear me in there?"

I blink at Cal. "Sorry. Lost in thought. You were saying something about the pre-PT program?"

"You mentioned math being a weak spot. I was just saying if you ever need help, you know, you're welcome to give me a call. I was king of the mathletes in high school."

I don't do as well at picking up on social cues as I used to, but I get the feeling he's flirting. Mostly it's the way that sandy mustache of his twitches at me in amusement.

"Okay, but listen, it's chemistry where I really struggled in high school and I don't mean that in any way that's flirty." Boy, that was graceful, wasn't it?

He looks around. Possibly planning an escape route. "It's getting late. You hungry?"

My stomach growls on my behalf. "Uh. It seems so. But…" I fiddle with the packet of admissions papers that we picked up earlier in the tour. "I should tell you, to be clear, that I'm kind of hung up on someone. I'm not good at this so I couldn't tell… I'm probably being an idiot. Never mind."

I put a cold hand on one hot cheek and turn away, heading in the direction of Pete's, which looks like an on-campus burger shop or something.

"Hey." Cal puts a hand on my shoulder. "For the record, you're not an idiot. Maybe I am, because you sort of already turned me down once and I should've known someone as cute as you would be taken. It's probably all for the best anyway, since if you get an internship on campus I'd end up sort of being your boss."

"That's right." I knock his hand away. "Stop hitting on the employees, perv."

God, I need to learn to leash my tongue. Luckily he starts laughing before I can find a hole to hide my head in.

He bumps my shoulder as we head into the place to get food. "So. Tell me about this guy of yours."

"Ugh. He's not really even mine. It's complicated."

"I love complicated. Or at least, I seem to be a magnet for it. My last relationship was with a married couple."

Halfway to the counter, I spin on my heel. "Whaaa-a-at?"

Ollie laughs harder. "I know. Nobody ever pegs me for a freak at first glance. Here. Let me buy you a burger and I'll tell you all about it."

I hit him in the shoulder. "No way. I'm nursing a broken heart and this is the most exciting thing I've heard all week. I'll buy lunch. You'll talk."

"Deal."

We wind up laughing with loaded burgers and frosted floats too cold for early April not to be absurd, but we go through most of my admissions paperwork, and it's the most human I've felt in a while.

I almost manage to ignore the hollow ache in my chest that tells me what an idiot I was for pushing Ty away.

Almost. But not quite.

20. SLOPPY HUG

Ty

"You sure about this, buddy?" Alonzo's with me in the locker room while Ernesto tapes my hands.

I shake my head. "Not entirely. But it's something I have to do."

Dante's across the room. In spite of telling me he couldn't be my trainer and didn't have the time to travel, he's been here for the big things. A rematch against ZZ was one thing he said he wouldn't miss.

Admittedly, I'm glad he's here.

"If the request had come quietly, we could've pushed it off. When you get called out publicly, it's harder to ignore. He would've looked like a pussy staying silent," Dante says.

Alonzo looks at me. "Better to look like a pussy than get your ass killed in the ring."

"I'm gonna be there to make sure that don't happen," Dante replies. "I've seen too many fights when the refs and the doctors didn't call it soon enough. If he's taking hits, I'll make sure they stop."

Alonzo isn't appeased. "You're sure—"

"I'll be fine." Frustration pushes me to my feet, but I sit just as fast.

The look on Alonzo's face is the same one on his face the morning he came to find me, saying we needed to make sure Kate was okay. Dude may party too hard, but he cares about his friends.

"You need to know something," he says quietly. A far more serious tone than I've ever heard from my best friend before.

"Do I need to know it now? It's about time to get my head in the right place."

He leans across from the bench he's sitting on. I know he's sober because I told him he had to be to come with us, but he looks ill and shaky, like he just woke up from a bender. "I knew what was going on with Terrence and that promoter."

"What the fuck?" Like that, I'm on my feet again, towering over Alonzo, and not caring this time about how my face looks. Or his. "What the hell did you know about Terrence that you didn't tell me?"

"I didn't tell anyone, okay? He told me not to. He promised me it was all under control. He did what he did for that guy, the guy gave him more favorable fight contracts supposedly, and the dude also promised to help set up your career since, you know…since you guys being in the system had messed with your training and whatnot."

I don't speak because I'm too shocked. Dante's standing next to me and I'm not sure when that happened, but he's not speaking either.

Alonzo looks up at both of us and licks his lips. "Terrence believed…he believed you really had what it took. Between the two of you. He thought you could go all the way if you wanted. He wanted to make it happen for you, and Arlo Specter told him he could." My friend's nostrils flare, his jaws clenched with anger. "But that sick fuck used him, and I didn't speak up, and Terrence died. So I have to say something now."

My chest is heaving. Disbelief and anger grapple inside of me. "How could you not have told me? Of all people. You were my friend. He was *my* brother—"

"And I loved him!" Alonzo explodes up to standing, pushing his nose against mine. "You and I may have been friends, but he and I were a hell of a lot more. So when he begged me not to tell, I didn't tell. Maybe if I had he'd still be alive. That's a mistake you don't see until it's too late. It's a mistake I have to live with. I'm sorrier than you'll ever know, believe me."

"I didn't know, man. I'm sorry." Jesus.

The three of us were in the same group home after Gran died. A few months in, I got sent to a different foster home. I knew Terrence and Alonzo were friends. They hung out, but I didn't realize…well, obviously there's a lot I didn't realize.

My head is spinning. I have to sit down.

No wonder Alonzo's been crazy since Terrence died. I guess I always thought… Now I'm not really sure what I thought.

"Hey. Alonzo." Dante steps up next to me, his voice cautious. "Maybe you can do something *now*. You know any specifics? Times? Places? What happened?"

Alonzo nods his head. "I know more than I wish I did."

"Would you be willing to talk to the DA? A guy I know is bringing a wrongful death suit for a guy who died in the ring under Arlo's management, but we're still trying to get enough evidence to bring charges for the young fighters he abused."

Alonzo sighs. "I'm not what people consider trustworthy, but if you think it can help, I'll try."

"That's all I ask. And listen." He puts a hand on Alonzo's shoulder. "I wouldn't let this kid see the inside of the octagon if he wasn't ready. We'll be watching. Your friend will be as safe as he can possibly be with a two-hundred-pound guy throwing punches at his face."

At that, Alonzo almost managed a smile.

"Hey, buddy. C'mere." I pull Alonzo into a sloppy hug.

Over his shoulder, Dante catches my eye and mouths, "We need to talk."

Yeah. We definitely did.

"You know, he blamed Kate for you losing that fight. To her face, blamed her."

Sigh. "Yeah. Wish I'd known a hell of a lot sooner."

"She believed him. You need to tell her it's not her fault."

"You're right, man. I do."

#

Kate

Without Ty around, it's easy to fall back on old habits. Bad habits. Ones that I fully acknowledge I can't keep doing forever.

I'm still not sleeping well, and more than that, I'm tired of thinking. In a few more days I can move into my new place, and while I'm still planning and moving forward, doing so is painful.

As I haul my new "bed" up the stairs of the B&B, in fact, my spirits sink a little. This was supposed to be a thing I did with Ty, not all alone. And it was supposed to be an actual bed, not one of those self-inflating air mattresses. I got to the store though and I couldn't justify the price and, *god*, the permanence of a real mattress.

What if I decide school isn't for me? Alonzo seems to be Team Ty these days. I like it here in Evergreen Grove, but I don't know what's keeping me exactly. Much as I'd love to hear more of Cal's sex stories.

Sierra catches me on the stairs, bringing down towels. "Oh, hey there, Kate. Need towels?"

This girl. She's so sweet and she tries so hard to be accommodating. A little too hard. I want to shake her and tell her to do things for herself, but I guess you can't do that when you work in the hospitality industry.

"I'm fine. I'm too tired to even shower tonight. All I want is to drag this box up to my room, pull the flat champagne out of my mini bar, and drink until I fall asleep."

I'm probably going to add a little white pill to help me sleep but I don't mention that to her.

"Oh. Let me help you there."

She jogs down a couple of stairs to a cabinet that contains fancy stemware. From a key on a scrunchy bracelet, she procures the means to open the bottom of the cabinet, and with a flourish, she whips out another one of those mini bottles.

"Don't tell anyone. We've actually got tons of these. Except for the occasional honeymooners—which, I mean, how many couples honeymoon in Evergreen Grove?—nobody drinks them."

"Oh. Wow. Thanks. You've totally made my night."

I end up showering after all once I get up to the room, rubbing my neck and feet with lotion in the shower the way Ty did for me, or trying to. Turns out when you only have your hand and you're doing it to yourself, it isn't nearly as effective.

The heat plus the valium help though, and I'm getting a little better at living with that hole in the center of my body. The way I figure it, I've survived having part of my face rebuilt and I had to spend half an hour trapped next to the dead brother of the boy I loved. Those were things I didn't think I'd come back from.

Now, the daily sadness sort of distracts me from the physical pain, but I manage to keep moving. I think it might be something I can get through, and for that I actually have Ty to thank.

Whenever I don't feel weird talking to him again.

My phone buzzes as I'm sipping my champagne from the bottle and wishing I could class it up with a straw. I don't feel like answering and it's probably Alonzo drunk-dialing me anyway.

"No, I do not want to hear about how epically you're about to get laid," I grumble at the phone.

Last weekend there was apparently a foursome. Two guys and two girls. I don't even know how that works with so many arms and legs. I'd get stage fright.

When the text messages start, I switch my phone to silent, bump up the thermostat, and climb under the covers. "If you need what-to-wear suggestions, you're barking up the wrong tree, Alonzo."

For the first time in a long time, I sleep in a blissful state of dead-to-the-world, until I wake sometime in the middle of the night to the sound of what I'm pretty sure is yelling.

I try to roll over and ignore it. Probably someone arguing out on the street or something. That used to happen back home. When I realize I have to go to the bathroom, I have no choice but to get out of bed, stumbling in nothing but an oversized T-shirt and boy shorts to the bathroom. I'm still hazy from the drugs and the alcohol but as I'm wobbling to the sink, I realize why it is that something doesn't feel right.

That light outside isn't dawn coming.

"Holy shit, the house next door is on fire."

I spin in a confused circle. Do I put on pants? Do I wash my hands? See, these are decisions I used to be better at making. Before.

Thumping down below. "Okay. Think."

I throw on one of the complimentary robes so I'm not running outside half naked and grab a towel, wetting it in the sink. I don't know what's going on down there but maybe it'll help. I jam my feet into the flimsy slippers that come with the room and I run down the stairs.

That friendly couple just passing through from the Outer Banks stumbles out, coughing. "There's smoke in our room," the wife gets out. The husband looks dazed.

"Okay. Out front."

"No. Wait. I can't go without Tubby."

"Who the hell is Tubby?" It's a bad time to think it, but her husband looks very Jack Sprat so I hope that isn't a nickname.

"My dog. He goes everywhere with me."

Oh dear Lord, she's one of those. "Okay, you know what? Your husband looks like he needs to get outside. Can you call 9-1-1?"

She holds up her phone.

"Great. I'm right behind you."

Their room is bigger than mine, with a Jacuzzi tub in the corner on a little platform. I find myself insanely making a mental note as I aim the flashlight from my phone around the dark corners calling, "Tubby, Tubby, where are yooou," like some kind of dork.

Trouble is, the smoke is building in here. From the looks of things outside the window, some of the bushes lining the house have caught from next door. Which means it's probably a matter of time before the house catches. "Okay, Tubby, get your little doggy ass out here so we can both stop breathing this smoke, okay?"

I lift up the dust ruffle of the bed, and there he is. Or at least, there are two glowing eyes staring out at me and it better damn well be a dog. Otherwise the fire isn't gonna be what kills me.

"Okay, Tubby. Whadya say, huh? Let's go and see the nice firemen before we all die? What do you think, huh, boy?" Totally guessing on the boy part.

I think back to my days of high school babysitting. Some of the families I worked with had dogs. They always got super obnoxious when you opened the door. Can't hurt to try.

"Hey, Tubby. Walk time, huh?"

Oh yeah. That perks him up.

"Yeah? That sound good? Let's get out from under this stuffy old bed and go for a walk. Maybe get a treat. Treat? You like treats, don't you, boy. Or girl. Or whatever. I don't judge. You be whatever you want to be, Tubby, so long as you come out from und—"

I get a face full of instant dog licks. "Oh, thank God. Tubby, it turns out, is some sort of curly-haired dachshund. "Let's get the hell out of here."

It's getting smokier in the room. I stick Tubby inside my bathroom and run for the door. Sierra passes us on the way, breathing into a tea towel and looking the way I imagine Martha Stewart would look escaping from a fire.

"Oh God, there you are, Kate! I was so worried about you guys."

"Had to stop and get a dog. Let's go."

It's chaos when we get outside. Most of the emergency-response folks are just showing up and their priority is the house next door.

"Kate. Hey!" Cal comes running up to me in his gear. "You okay?"

"Freezing. But yeah. I'm not sure about this little guy." I hold up the dog. His owners don't seem to be present at the moment.

"Do me a favor, go and get checked out and then stay over there. I'll be by later."

We go, and Tubby scrambles inside the collar of my shirt looking for warmth. I can't blame him. "I know, Tubby, that's a comfortable shirt. But don't get too settled. Just as soon as everything starts to feel good, you'll have to say goodbye."

I miss Ty. As I stare up at the house next door, this huge fancy house that's being reduced to nothing but charred boards in front of my eyes, I feel his loss so much it hurts. If something so big and sturdy had no hope, what hope do he and I have? And yet, I let my fear cloud my judgment and I'm pretty sure there are better ways I could've handled things with him.

I don't know what he's doing tonight. Who he's with, for that matter. But I could at least text him and tell him. I could, except I don't have my phone. I must have dropped it after I found Tubby.

Sierra taps me on the shoulder. "Hey, you okay?"

"Yeah." All I can do now is stand by and watch, once again a passenger while things burn around me.

Until I remember my backpack. The pictures inside. They're upstairs, and they're all I have left of Ty.

"Wait." I hand Tubby off to a startled Sierra. "See if you can find his owners. I'll be right back."

"Kate, you can't go back in there!"

I'm already running.

#

Ty

"Hey, it's me. You're not answering your phone and I'm about to go out there and maybe I'll win or maybe I won't, but I wanted you to know that nothing that happens to me in that octagon is your fault. Terrence never should have laid that at your feet, and I…I really should have done better at letting you know where we stood. I hope we can talk soon."

It's the fastest fight of my life. We don't touch gloves and ZZ comes out swinging.

Adrenaline is white lightning in my veins. We're grappling before I can count the seconds, him trying to pin me and me twisting and flipping to try to get the better of him.

Sweat pours. My skin chafes from the time on the mat. He puts good effort into keeping my left arm pinned, shooting pain through my neck and shoulder. It wears me out but it also pisses me off.

So much that I twist away and let my fist fly, landing a lucky shot that stuns him. One more and he's down, landing gracefully on that mat since he didn't have far to fall. Me, I'm standing there with my heart racing so hard I can't believe it's all over.

Not the fastest KO in history, but in the end all of that wrestling on the floor only lasted about two and a half minutes. I'll take it.

Damn right I will.

ZZ's angry and already yelling about a rematch before I leave. I didn't expect this thing to be televised, but I guess it was on some cable channel somewhere. There are microphones in my face, and people want me to answer crazy questions like whether or not I expected to win.

I'm sure I'm supposed to do a bunch of posturing and shouting about how I'm gonna come in and kick ass and take names. That's what I see most guys doing. Instead, I'm so taken off guard that I say, "No way, man. I was lucky to beat 'im."

That really seems to stir up the reporters.

Thankfully, Dante comes and pulls me out of there, saving me from further embarrassment. I'm looking forward to heading home tonight. If I drive back with Alonzo, I can get a decent night's sleep and go see Kate after breakfast. Hopefully she'll be feeling forgiving and I can extend an olive branch by offering once again to help her move. And meaning it this time.

Something's wrong when I get to the dressing room. Far from the celebratory mood of before, Alonzo is solemn. Dante is pacing again.

"What's going on, guys?"

"Have a seat." Dante points to the bench.

"I hear just as well standing up."

Alonzo shakes his head. "Fuck. He's trying to be classy about it, shit. A guy I know is on the volunteer rescue squad or whatever. He sent me a text, there's a fire over at the Radcliffe mansion. It's literally right next to the inn where Kate's been staying."

Dante turns his head. "I don't suppose she's moved yet?"

"No. she's supposed to do it in a couple of days."

"All right." Dante claps me on the shoulder. "Probably fine. After all, they said next door. Let's get you on the road just in case."

For a second I'm frozen, before the slam of Dante pulling my stuff out of my locker puts me in gear. "Yeah."

Yeah. That's right. I have to move. Get dressed. Get on the road.

Try not to think about what would happen if I lost Kate again. Because that's not an option. I lost her once. I can't lose her again.

21. FLORENCE NIGHTINGALE

Ty

Some moments in my life have cut me off at the knees. Hearing about my brother. Seeing Kate in the hospital, looking barely alive.

The moment when Dante pulls us up a block away from the fire, I can still move but I feel more like I got lifted up and socked in the face. Maybe it's because I recognize Kate as soon as I jump from his Jeep—and what I see isn't good.

She's out. She's alive, at the very least. But they're rolling her on one of those gurneys toward a waiting ambulance.

Until someone stops me, I don't even realize I've been calling her name. A guy in fireman gear leans down to wave his hand in my face. He's got her backpack—the old Jansport she's had since school—but that doesn't make any sense.

"What the hell are you doing with her stuff?"

"Hey. Relax. Breathe. I'm pretty sure she's okay, but she went back in for it so they're treating her for smoke inhalation. She needs to go to the hospital to get checked out. Are you Tyler?"

That straightens me up. "Yeah. You are?"

He slaps a hand on my back and shoves the backpack against my chest. "Cal. I'm a friend. I've been helping Kate get her enrollment package together for school. She's pretty great."

My fingers curl tight and angry around the loop of the pack. "You don't need to tell me."

Now run along. Let me go see for myself that she's okay.

"Right. So they'll be taking her to St. John's."

"I know where that is," Dante says from behind me. "My mom's a frequent flier."

"Thanks."

I'm antsy the whole ride, shuffling my feet and muttering. I try to call but her phone goes straight to voice mail. Guess it gets bad, because Alonzo puts his hands on my shoulders, tightening them like clamps.

"Dude. She's going to be all right. You gotta calm down."

"Can't make any assumptions."

"No. You can't. And until you know, there's no reason to freak out."

"Your easy-bake friend over here has a point."

Alonzo glares at the back of Dante's head with his best "fuck off" glare but doesn't say anything.

"Yeah," I say. "You're right. It's going to be fine."

Except they make us wait several minutes when we finally get there.

"They're probably just examining her," Dante offers.

"Or something bad happened."

"Or they're just examining her."

Alonzo shakes his head.

I walk the length of the desk, looking for someone to fight. A bored-looking grandpa behind the desk pecks away at a keyboard while a few feet away, some lady struggles with what sounds like a stomach virus.

Dante cringes and scoots away. "Man, I will be in so much trouble if I bring sick germs home."

I can't help it. That cracks me up. "Dante Ramos. Whipped by his fiancée?"

He puffs his chest out all big and proud. "Damn right. You find yourself the right person to love, a whipped man is a happy man. You mark my words."

The woman over in the waiting area retches into a bedpan someone's given her to hold.

"Oh geez," Alonzo mutters. "This is terrible. We've been here twenty minutes and nobody's checking on her. I'm gonna keep her company for a while."

"You don't know what she has, man. You sure?" I put a hand on his arm for a second but then let it drop again. Alonzo's a big boy and I'm worried about other things.

"Please. Six roommates? Someone's always got mono or the flu or legionnaire's disease or something. Rock-solid immune system right here." He shrugs me off and goes to sit down beside the lady, offering her some tissues, which is a nice gesture.

"That's gonna bite him in the ass someday, thinking he's invincible," Dante says.

"Uh-huh." I clap my hands together. "He's a good guy, though. Cares about people. Be better if he could stop fucking around long enough to care about himself."

"That takes a while for some folks."

"I know that's right." My own self included.

"Hey, there you guys are."

Kate's voice brings my head around. Standing in an open set of double doors in blue-green hospital scrubs, she looks tired but happy to see us.

I'm thankful for that last part, because I can't keep myself off her when she comes through the door. "There *you* are, you mean. We've been waiting."

"Oh. I didn't know, sorry. They told me someone was here but not who. Or where. I kept waiting for you to come back to where I was."

I glare at the grandpa who made us wait. Convenient how he's engrossed in a book of Sudoku puzzles. "Well, here we are." I'm patting her arms, looking her up and down to be sure she's all right. "What's going on? You have to stay for tests or observation or anything?"

"Nope. They wanted me to get some oxygen and check my vitals. Honestly, I'm not sure they needed to bring me here. That poor elderly lady from next door to the B&B was way worse. She was the one who started the fire next door. Knocked over a candle and couldn't see where it landed."

"I'm just glad to see you in one piece." I hand over her backpack. "One of the firemen said you went back in for this. If you promise never to do that again, I won't give you anymore trouble about your pain meds."

She presses her lips together in an intense line. "My prescriptions were in the bathroom. I didn't go back for those. I went back for these." She pulls out an old notebook. The single-subject, spiral-bound kind you get in school, with all kinds of scribbles and stickers on the front. She opens it up, and…

"Holy cow."

Inside, she's pasted all sorts of shit about me. Or us, I guess. Pictures of me as a kid. Pictures of us together on those little trips she dragged me on. Pictures she took of me fighting. Pictures of me and my twin at our gran's grave on Thanksgiving.

"Where'd all these come from?"

"Some of them I'm sure you remember. Your brother had a box of stuff. The childhood pictures are from there. I grabbed a couple of things out of there one day when you guys weren't paying attention. I kept them, and after the accident I found them in one of my books. They helped me remember you. When everything in my head was so foggy after the accident. You were my anchor to reality." She swallows.

Over by the main entrance to the ER, I hear a whistling noise as Dante makes himself scarce.

"Funny. You weren't too happy to see me when we found you at that party. Thought you'd given up on me."

She shook her head. "You weren't either though. And it was hard. After all the things Terrence said. He told me I wasn't good enough for you about thirty seconds before we crashed. Ty, I'm so sorry but… I'll never be sure he didn't do it on purpose. I may not have remembered consciously, but every time I looked at you, the fear and everything came up I think."

Holy hell. Her revalation about Terrence clamps my eyes shut. It hurts to think he'd do such a thing. It hurts more to think I didn't know how to help him out of such a dark place. Worse yet, that he almost took Kate with him.

I pull her toward me. "It was my fault. All the things he said about you, I let him believe them because he and I had forgotten how to talk to each other. I should have set him straight. The stuff going on with his coach. I should've said something. I wanted to, but I didn't know how. Bottom line, I wish I had done more. Been better."

"You can't have been expected to handle something like that. I didn't know what to say either."

"He told you?" Disbelief rocks me back.

"Right before the accident. I didn't remember until recently."

"Shit. I can't believe he told you."

"I think he was trying to… You know. Shock me. I don't know."

I hate to think about what would have happened if Terrence had gotten his way. As much as I loved my brother, there's no denying he was troubled. "I'd like to think if Terrence were around, he'd have eventually seen the light. He'd love you as much as I do." I squeeze both of her hands. "Did you get my messages?"

She shakes her head. "I dropped my phone somewhere when we were getting out of the fire."

Oh. "Well the gist was, I'm sorry and I love you."

Her eyes widen and her lips come apart. "You do?"

"Come on, girl. I've loved you since you told me it wasn't your problem the library was right up the street from where we held our fights."

She pushes her head against my chest. "God, that was goofy."

"Nah. This is goofy." I flip to the picture of me in her notebook, taken on picture day when I was in the fourth grade. I'd picked my clothes so carefully; my gran had ironed my button-down shirt and khaki pants, which I'd carefully paired with my favorite *Star Trek* belt.

"Aww. I love that picture. And you and Spock clearly had a thing."

"Hey, I ain't even trying to mess with you if you can't rock a Spock belt."

She hugs the notebook to her chest and laughs, but quickly starts coughing a little.

"All right," I say. "Let's get serious here." My hands go to her shoulders, squeezing tight. "I thought I'd lost you tonight. My fight went well, I got out of there, and the only person I wanted to share it with was you. Then I found out there had been a fire and I almost lost my mind."

"I'm okay, Ty."

"But I didn't know. For all I knew, I'd lost my chance with you by letting that BS about me not sleeping piss me off enough to make me leave."

"It wasn't BS. I wanted to—"

"Protect me, I know. We're going to work that out. I'm going to wait a few months before I sign another contract, and you and I are gonna get you set up in your new place. I hear it has a bedroom and a living room. I have trouble sleeping, I can crash on the couch or at Alonzo's. But I know it won't be a problem because we're going to get you some help for those nightmares."

Her lips curve up. "Did you just invite yourself to move in with me?"

"Baby, weren't you there? My name's on the lease. You trying to say you don't want me with you?"

She laughs and sputters again. "Okay. Stop making me laugh. Yes, I want you there. I do."

"All right then, all settled."

Her eyes open wide. "Oh God. No, it isn't."

"What's the problem?"

"Where do we sleep tonight? My new place isn't ready for two more days and the place where I was sleeping just caught fire."

"I guess we could go to Alonzo's." Except I sleep on a cot that barely fits me, let alone two people.

Dante wanders back inside. He's been talking with someone on the phone but puts it away when the old dude at the counter glares at him. Sure, no time to let me back to see my girl or get that puking woman a room, but cell phone use he's on top of.

"Yo, Champ." Dante tosses something shiny and I catch it before I can see that I'm holding a key. "Stay at my place tonight. Be sure to feed my dog and walk him or I'll kill you."

"What about you and your pussy-whipping girlfriend? Will she mind?"

"I don't think that's— Whatever. Michelle's working on a project. She's setting up some kind of show on campus so she's been coming home late and crashing hard. She'll be fine."

"You sure?"

"Yeah. Get out of here before I change my mind. You can take the connector bus." He nods in the direction of Alonzo and the new friend he's made. "I'll make sure Florence Nightingale over there gets home unscathed."

I look at Kate. "You ready? You good?"

"I'm more than good. I'm amazing."

"You do look pretty hot in those scrubs."

"Okay, stop. Let's go."

"Don't anybody use my toothbrush," Dante calls after us.

#

Kate

There's a big guy in a tuxedo at my door.

A big. Huge. Hot. Guy in a tuxedo. One that stretches perfectly across every muscle and accentuates every movement. If this garment ripped from the strain of

Ty's curled arm, I think it would make the sacrifice happily.

"You look absolutely amazing," he says between kisses.

I lift onto my toes and kiss him back, feeling a twinge of discomfort in my neck but it's been better lately. I'm learning to enjoy things rather than bracing for impact. Right now I'd rather focus on the cool scent of his aftershave and the minty taste of his breath. The warmth of his tongue.

"I was about to say that same thing to you," I tell him when he finally lets me back down to the floor. "You know, I don't think I've ever seen you like this. You're so…"

"Stiff?"

"Ha. I was going to say handsome. You are every day, but the tux definitely adds a little something."

"Hmm. This have something to do with why you're always watching Batman movies?"

"I watch all kinds of movies."

Except I really do love a sharply dressed Bruce Wayne. As in, a lot.

"So where are we going?"

"You'll see. But first…"

Holy bleep, it's a wrist corsage. "You didn't."

"It's long overdue," he murmurs. "Never did get to take you to the prom."

This brings an inexplicable rush of moisture to my eyes. Our missed prom date was almost two years ago, but I'm still sad we didn't get to go. I guess it feels nice that he wishes we had, too.

He takes a step back, holding my hand as he looks me up and down. When I was told to dress up, I didn't know quite what to expect. I was worried I'd gone overboard. Now, I'm glad I chose what I did. A black beaded dress with spaghetti straps that I'd bought on a whim at the local thrift shop, hoping maybe someday I'd have an excuse to put it on.

"I can't wait to see what that dress looks like on the floor." The predatory gleam in his eye makes me shiver.

"Should we skip dinner?"

"Hell no. Had to kiss some ass to get this reservation."

We drive to dinner in a really nice Mustang. "Wow. Have I seen this car before?"

He laughs. "We borrowed it from your drummer the night we kidnapped you from Aspiration. You were too drunk to remember. He apparently never loans his car to anyone, so we owe him bigtime after all of this."

"I'll have to send him a nice fruit basket."

"You seen the fridge in Alonzo's place? It's where fruit goes to turn evil."

Turns out he made us reservations at the Heart and Hearth, an old farmhouse turned into a restaurant that I've heard is the town's one super-nice restaurant. And boy is it ever.

Low lighting, burnished wood, and savory food smells greet us when we walk in the door. The hostess seats us without blinking an eye, the waiter brings us bread and comments on our prom attire without surprise, which is when I realize a whole lot of young people around us are dressed similarly.

"Uh, Ty?"

"Yeah. Grove High is having their prom tonight. Like I said, I had a hell of a time getting a table here."

"We're not going to Grove High's prom, are we?"

He laughs. "No, but don't think I didn't ask. Turns out one person in your pair has to be a student."

I roll my eyes. "Stupid rules."

"I'm saying."

It's hard to eat dinner with the nervous butterflies in my stomach. My shrimp and avocado salad is delicious but too much for all the questions swirling in my head. Where are we going tonight and why is he being so mysterious?

Across from me, Ty is tucking into a slab of meatloaf (with extra gravy) so enthusiastically it's almost comical. "Damn. This is good. For real. You need to try this."

"I don't know. It looks a little heavy and I'm not really—"

"Come on. There's mushrooms in the gravy. Don't sleep on these mushrooms."

"Bring it in, big guy."

He's feeding me a bite, and yes it is delicious, when our hostess walks by with an old-style instant camera to take our picture.

"Happy prom night, kids!"

Ty laughs. "Kids. Like we're all twelve."

I tip my head. "I *am* still pretty young. And I'm definitely younger than you. You ever worry this thing won't work out?"

He forks up mashed potatoes. More gravy. I worry for a moment that he has to think about the question. Then I realize he's looking at the picture our hostess took. Him smiling with his fork out, me looking startled.

"You see this? I've been waiting years for this. 'Til you were old enough and was sure I had a life I could offer you." He shakes his head. "We've stumbled a couple of times but I'm not going anywhere. You?"

"No."

"Good. Now are we getting dessert or getting out of here?"

"Out. I need to know where we're going."

"You better like it."

"You'll be there, won't you?"

He grins and signals for the check.

Our next destination is an even bigger surprise. "Uh, Ty? Is this a gay bar? There's a sign that says it's 'Twinks and Bears' night on Tuesday."

The thumping music. The neon lights. The posters of shirtless men. It all screams…well, not the sort of place you'd go wearing a tuxedo.

"Is that what this place is?" He's not hiding his smile very well. "Crazy. Let's check it out inside."

We get inside and I'm blown away. "Holy shit." There are balloons and glittery stars hanging from the ceiling. Fairly lights strung around the room. Streamers. Someone went to the trouble of decorating the place just like a high school gym for a dance.

"It looks like a…"

"Prom?"

I'm struck dumb, so I only nod and look around the room. There's a drag queen at the bar serving fancy little cocktails and a table with cookies and punch.

The DJ is spinning eighties music and a few well-dressed people are out on the dance floor kicking balloons. Some look to be about my age. Some are clearly older. Twenties. Thirties. There are even a couple of men dancing with gray hair.

"Ohmygawd. This is awesome. How did you even hear about this?"

"Tyler, glad you could make it."

"Hey." Ty reaches out to shake hands with a tall blond guy and his companion, a handsome model-looking dude in a tux that definitely isn't rented.

Ty taps my shoulder. "Kate, this is AJ and his partner Hayden. Their daughter is in my class at the gym. He told me about the event here."

AJ nods. "They do this every year. Same night as the local proms. Safe-space alternative, and all that. Less of an issue than it used to be, but adults like to come so it's a good time for everybody. This is our first year, actually."

"Well it's awesome. Thank you."

"You bet." He tugs on his partner's hand. "We'll see you out on the dance floor, I hope."

Someone taps Ty on the shoulder. I recognize the handsome uniformed officer from the Sherriff's station as Lieutenant Haas, who looks a bit out of place in his uniform.

"Hey, folks. Sorry to interrupt."

"Eeeey, Haas! Have some punch!" Alonzo sidles up with a cup filled with some suspicious liquid.

Haas shakes his head. "I just came by to let you guys know we got the guys who tossed the brick into Delia's window. Turns out a kid from Grove High got his heart broken, and when he saw his ex holding hands with someone else through the bakery window he decided to get even."

Geez. "Small towns, huh?"

Haas nods. "Next to petty theft and speeding tickets, I spend more time on domestic disputes than about anything else."

In this quaint little town? Hard to imagine.

Haas turns to Alonzo and his strange, red drink. "Alonzo, I don't want to have to stick you in the drunk tank again."

"Relax, LT. It's orange soda mixed with fruit punch."

Lieutenant Haas gives Alonzo a look of suspicion. "Uh-huh. Just be careful. You folks have a good night."

Alonzo looks insulted, but shakes it off in his usual fashion. "I think that asshole didn't believe me. Fuck him, imma go dance."

I slide my arms around Ty's waist. "Well. Should we?"

"You want punch first?"

"I only want you."

I could stare forever at the look on his face.

The DJ starts up a slow song and I press my cheek to his chest. "I never thought I'd enjoy the high school sway so much in my life."

He chuckles. "Sorry. Never got around to those ballroom dancing lessons."

"I'm not."

"Hey. Got something to ask you."

"Ask anything." There's nothing I wouldn't do for him. I was willing to let him go if it meant his happiness. So whatever it is, my answer is yes.

"Well…I've been thinking it might be a lot for you, but it's coming up on the anniversary."

Of the accident. Terrence's death.

"I know."

"Don't know about you, but the last one—the first one—was hard for me. I've been wanting to go back home. Visit where Terrence was buried. I've made a little bit of money, so I could finally put up a proper headstone."

Oh, Ty. "Honey." My arms go around his neck and I press a kiss to his cheek. "That's something you never need to ask of me. I'm always there for you for that stuff."

"You were in that wreck next to him. I didn't want to make it hard for you."

"But *you'll* be next to me now. We're going to get through it together. Like you said."

He closes his eyes. "Yeah."

"Can I ask one favor also?"

"Ask anything."

"When we go home to see your brother, I think I should visit my mom. Let her know I'm okay."

"I think someone smart and handsome suggested that to you a while ago."

"Yeah. Well I always listen to you, even if sometimes I'm slow."

"Of course we'll go see your mom."

"I hope she's okay. You think she's going to be mad?" Because let's be honest. I may be mad at my mother for a lot, but she's still my mom.

"I think she'll be glad to know you're doing well."

And if she's not, well then that'll be that, won't it?

"By the way," Ty whispers in my ear. "You forgot to tell me about something. I saw the admissions letter on the table by the couch."

"Yesss. I was waiting to tell you and then you blew me away with all of this." I didn't mean to keep it a secret. Really. But then I got to go to the prom.

"Congratulations, baby. Looks like we got a lot to celebrate."

"We do. Most of all, each other."

"Hell yeah." We dance together for a minute, his finger sliding back and forth under the strap of my dress. "Still looking forward to getting this off you when we get home."

I laugh. "I'm looking forward to that, too," I say as I press my lips to his. "Thank you for this, Ty. I love you."

"Anything, baby. I love you, too."

Anything. I believe it. As long as we have each other, we can never lose.

THANK YOU for reading LOSING THE FIGHT! Reviews help readers find stories. Please take a few seconds to leave a an honest review of this or any other books you've read lately. To keep up with this series and all my other shenanigans, please sign up for my newsletter (tiny.cc/StaabNews).

Other books in The Evergreen Grove Series

At the Stars

Acts of Creation

By the Rules

Piece by Piece

About Elisabeth

Elisabeth Staab loves passionate stories and happy endings. Her books have been called "sexually charged," "action-packed," and "gloriously snarky." When not writing romance about vampires and werewolves and CEOs (oh, my!), she enjoys date night with her husband, playing UNO with her kids, and marathoning her favorite books or TV series. Find out more at ElisabethStaab.com.

Acknowledgements

I always have to thank my readers first, because without you this writing thing wouldn't be nearly as fun. Thanks especially to the Staab Mob for the pimpage and the book chat and for generally being lots of fun.

HUGE thank you to Kelli Collins for editing. I always appreciate your awesome insight. Thanks also to Jena at Practical Proofing and Angela Quarles at Geek Girl Author Services for polishing and swaddling this baby so it could look its best. So much gratitude to Elizabeth Babski for the cover design, to the fine folks at Period Images, and of course to Sean Hampton for being hot AF. ;)

I owe a huge debt of gratitude and about a thousand glasses of wine to Amber Belldene, Robin Covington, and Kristin Miller for helping me to make sure that Losing the Fight was the best it could be. For checking my assumptions and factual inaccuracies, and most of all for cheering me on when I needed it most. Thanks, ladies, for being the absolute best. (Any and all remaining mistakes are absolutely my own fault and nobody else's.)

To Tom, I wouldn't, *couldn't*, do any of it without you. This book was written in the middle of an interstate move, and unimaginable insanity. Thanks for always being my rock.

70475854R00141

Made in the USA
Columbia, SC
07 May 2017